Grace's Turn

Grace's Turn

Christy Carlson Romano

HYPERION BOOKS FOR CHILDREN
New York

First Edition
1   3   5   7   9   10   8   6   4   2

Designed by Angela Corbo Gier
Printed in the United States of America
Reinforced binding
This book is set in 11/17 Baskerville BT.
Library of Congress Cataloging-in-Publication Data on file.
ISBN 0-7868-4884-7

Visit www.hyperionbooksforchildren.com

To my family,
who weren't afraid of
loving all of me

Chapter One

The weekend before school starts, my best friend, Emily, comes over.

"About time, Grace!" she says when I open the door. "I thought you were never coming back from that summer camp."

"It was *theater school*," I tell her. We troop up the stairs to my bedroom. "We weren't paddling canoes or toasting marshmallows around the campfire. We were rehearsing dance numbers and learning vocal exercises and—"

"Whatever," says Emily. "If there's bad food, bunk beds, and weird boys, it's camp."

She's right, but I don't tell her that. Emily's not here to talk about camp anyway. She's here for what she calls an Important Junior Year Strategy Meeting. Emily's determined to break into the A-list at Cumberland High. I lie on my bed, using Oscar—my old and much-loved teddy bear—to prop up my head. Emily sits on my desk with her legs dangling, her flip-flops dropping to the floor.

"Okay, G." Emily hardly ever calls me Grace. "This is the year we're gonna do it."

"I doubt it," I tell her, rolling my eyes. The A-list is made up of girls with great teeth and glossy hair who organize things, and guys who are star athletes and wear the collars of their polo shirts turned up. We don't fit into either category. We're drama club girls, not fashion plates or sports heroes. But Emily refuses to accept exile from the A-list.

"Nice attitude." She frowns. "Let's review the situation. First, what improvements have we made on ourselves this summer?"

"Braces off," I say, sighing with relief. I am no longer the oldest-ever-girl-to-still-have-braces at Cumberland High School. My father is a dentist, so he's a nut about each of his three kids having perfect teeth.

"What else?" Emily clicks her fingers.

"And my singing has improved, I guess," I say. "Or no, maybe my acting . . ."

"Stop right there!" Emily shrieks. She can be pretty fierce at times, even though she looks more like a Goody Two-shoes at the moment because she's blow-dried her red hair into a shoulder-length flip. "Braces off—that's good. But singing and acting—they don't care!"

"Who doesn't care?"

"Hell-o! The A-list! The in-crowd! The Blueblood Lobsters!"

Our school football team is known as the Blue Lobsters. Our town—Cumberland, Connecticut—is famous for the rare blue lobster someone here caught eons ago, which means every second entry in the Yellow Pages is called Blue Lobster something. My brother even calls our family car the Blue Lobster Cadillac. It's a pretty lame thing to be famous for, but Cumberland milks it to death.

"My dancing has really improved, too," I tell Emily.

She rolls her eyes. "What are you planning to do—tap-dance down the halls of Cumberland High singing 'I Got Rhythm' and hope your spirit-fingers win the A-list over?"

"I don't care about them," I tell Emily, pulling Oscar out from behind my head and throwing him at her. She ducks just in time, so poor Oscar bounces off my Audrey Hepburn poster and falls to the floor. Audrey is my idol, and Emily's crazy about her as well. Whenever we're stuck on a problem—like deciding which pair of jeans to buy, or which guy on *The OC* to obsess over—we ask each other, "What would Audrey do?"

"Dude, don't even think of dragging Audrey into this," Emily warns me. We spend so much time together, she can read my mind. "I'm glad I called this meeting

3

before school starts and things go *seriously* awry. To think I was going to wait until Monday lunchtime!"

"So tell me," I say, sitting up. "What improvements have *you* made this summer?"

"I'm glad you asked." She pretends to smooth out the wrinkles in her capri pants. "I have accomplished the following: One, I can now iron my hair straight and curl the ends in under fifteen minutes."

"You must be so proud," I mock.

"Two, and thanks for not noticing, I've lost weight. Not a lot, but it's a start."

This is something that's been driving Emily crazy for the last year, even though my mother told her it was just puppy fat and nothing to worry about. Emily says she doesn't want to be a puppy. If she has to be a baby animal at all, she wants to be something lean and mean but still cute, like a young cheetah.

"Three, I've been taking a ton of photographs."

"That's great, Em, but how does it help you infiltrate the A-list?" Photography has been Emily's hobby for a while. She says her favorite subject is Rascal, my family's husky, because he sits still on command and doesn't complain if the finished product is unflattering.

"I knew you wouldn't be able to see the bigger picture—no pun intended," she drawls. "I'll simplify it for you. I take my portfolio to the school paper. They beg me to take pictures at sports games. I get total access to A-listers, on the field, in the locker room. They beg me to take pictures at school dances and the Blue Lobster pep rallies. I get access to A-listers on the committee. Soon they'll want me at their parties, taking pictures of them getting ready, hanging out . . . Get it now?"

"But you don't even like sports!" I protest. "And you think the Blue Lobster pep rallies are stupid! Last year you wore green to every one to symbolize how they made you sick! I remember you sitting here in this very room asking, 'What would Audrey do?' And you decided she wouldn't be seen dead in a Blue Lobster T-shirt!"

"True," sighs Emily. She turns around to stroke the poster, running one finger down Audrey's slim black dress. "But we have to face facts, G. When Audrey was growing up, she was, like, a ballerina in Belgium. She was never a junior at Cumberland High. And anyway, nobody says I have to enjoy myself taking pictures at school events. Sometimes you have to suffer for your art."

"And for the chance to hang out with A-listers," I point out.

"That's just a bonus," she sniffs. "I'm doing this for you, too, by the way. I'll open the doors and you can dance right through, spirit-fingers and all."

"Thanks—but let me get this straight. Your plan is to become, like, the paparazzi."

"A *paparazza*, thank you very much. Not bad, eh?"

"But presuming your evil plan works, how will you still have time for drama club?"

"Sure, I'll still be a theater geek—on the down low. But let's get back to you. You need a plan."

"I have a plan," I tell her, stretching my arms and yawning. "Try to get good grades, do well on the PSAT, start studying for the SAT—"

"Where are your priorities?" Emily groans, slapping her forehead.

"And try to get a feature role in the school musical. For the first time ever. Even if I get a small part, that's going to keep me pretty busy in the spring semester."

"You know, G," says Emily, giving me one of her long, scrutinizing stares, "you don't have to be *just* a theater geek. You can be, you know, a cool chick, too. What you need to do is go for the lead in the musical and get it—"

"Are you out of your mind? We don't even know what show they've picked, and I've only ever been in the chorus."

"So? There has to be a first time for everything. You think Vanessa Williams never sweated it out as a scenery-hugger? You think Kristin Chenoweth didn't start out small?"

"She *is* small. She's even smaller than you."

Emily gives a deep, you're-driving-me-crazy sigh.

"Dude, I meant in small *roles*. What I'm saying is, if Kristin was at Blue Lobster High, she wouldn't have scored the lead in her sophomore year, no matter how totally talented she was, or how she aced the audition. They would still have given it to that fem-bot Terri Cooper just because she's a platinum blonde and her mother raised all the money for the new auditorium."

"I guess," I say, lying down again and flexing my ankles. "But Terri's pretty good, you know."

"You're better," says Emily, and then she lowers her voice so it sounds like she's asking me on some top-secret mission. "You have to promise me. If this is going to be our year, we have to go for it. *You* have to go for it."

"Can't next year be our year?" I plead.

"Dude, next year is the backup plan," says Emily. She thinks of everything. "If we leave it till next year, and things don't work out then, we'll go through the rest of our lives looking back at high school with bitterness and regret. So it's all or nothing—are we agreed?"

"I guess," I tell her, but I don't sound too enthusiastic, so she slides down from the desk, scoops up Oscar off the floor, and pelts me with him. "Okay! Okay! All or nothing."

"We have to get ourselves out there, G. I'm serious."

"Just one question," I say. "What if I don't get the lead role in the musical—whatever it is?"

"Plan B," she says.

"And what's Plan B?"

"I haven't got the details sorted out yet, but it's either you become a cheerleader, or we go to South America as exchange students."

"Emily!"

"I'm telling you, it's got to be something drastic. I can't take another year of social obscurity. The only people who invite us to parties are boys who spend their summers at computer camp rewriting Dungeons & Dragons. Boys who are shorter than I am. Do you hear me, G? *Boys who are shorter than I am.* We can't go on like this. It has to be all or nothing."

So I agree to all or nothing—to make Emily happy— and because, even though her plans are crazy, I know she's right. Why shouldn't this be my year?

After Emily goes home to get her clothes and books ready for the first day of school tomorrow, I stand looking around my room more critically than usual. It's the smallest bedroom in the house, and I've always loved its coziness and the way it looks out over trees and the front yard. A white chair sits near the window, where I like to curl up with a book. My old ballet slippers dangle from the bulletin board above my desk. It's still a pretty room, and a comfortable room, but suddenly it strikes me as being a little girl's room, not really mine.

"Dinner's ready!" my mother shouts up the stairs, and I hurry to pull my hair into a ponytail.

My brother, Tom, pokes his head around the door. "Last one downstairs has to help clean up," he says. Tom acts as though he's about six years old, but he's actually a year older than me—fifteen months and three weeks older, to be precise. He and my sister, Sonia, are twins. Everyone says that only my parents would be crazy enough to have another baby just a year after having twins. Especially twins like Sonia and Tom, or Good and Evil, as they're known in the family. Sonia has always been the good girl, and Tom, bratty and boisterous. They haven't changed much, even though they're about to become seniors in high school.

"I already checked the roster on the fridge," I tell him. "It's your turn, idiot."

"On second thought, maybe you should skip dinner tonight." He looks me up and down, a mock frown on his face. "I mean, you've really piled on a lot of weight this summer."

I make a face at him and give his arm a not-so-playful punch.

"Very funny!" I say, brushing past him and heading for the stairs. He runs after me, grabbing me on the landing and trying to tickle me. "Get off! You're so immature. I can't believe you're going to be a senior this year."

"Neither can I," he says, and pushes me out of the way so he can race to the table first. "Look out, everyone! Little Gracie's not so little anymore!"

I stick my nose in the air and attempt to walk to the table in a dignified and elegant manner, as though I'm Audrey Hepburn and not "Little Gracie." Apart from stepping on a dog toy, which lets out a startling squeak, and tripping over the edge of the rug, I don't do too badly. Anyway, nobody would notice if I fell on my face: they're already sitting around the table, helping themselves to huge bowls of pasta and talking nonstop. I forget about trying to look elegant and rush over to my chair. Growing up and getting serious can wait until tomorrow, when I'm back in school.

Chapter Two

School begins, and the whole "all or nothing" plan gets shelved for a few days. Emily and I have new classes to settle into, new teachers to get along with, heavy new books to stack in our lockers. There's a special meeting for all juniors so we can get lectured about test preparation and choosing a college. Unlike my brother, I do take this kind of thing seriously—but unlike my sister, who's kind of a brainiac, I can't really get excited over it. College seems like an eternity away right now.

Cumberland High isn't the worst place to go to school, though it's not really like those high schools on TV. By that I mean nobody really dresses up in high fashion or drives their own BMW. It's not easy to be cool when your school team is called the Blue Lobsters. For a while we tried to make them sound better by calling them the B-Lobs, but then all the other teams dubbed us the Blobs, and any attempt at cool was over, once and for all.

On the first Friday back, Mr. Thomas, the principal, holds an all-school assembly in the gym. Most of it's the usual stuff. Coach Furtado tries to get us excited about the start of the football season, getting all red-faced and hoarse, like he's about to have a heart attack. Mr. Greer, the science teacher with hair that sprouts in patches all over his bald head like cacti growing in a desert, drones on about this year's senior project for the national science fair. Ms. Schaeffer, the cheerleader who never grew up, shrieks about the Blue Lobster pep rallies and how they're going to be THE BEST EVER, which is exactly what she said last year, and the year before. She points out some of the A-list girls—the ones who spend every fall semester walking around carrying clipboards and IMing each other and flashing brilliant smiles at anyone who buys tickets for rally events—and they jump up and wave to everyone, until Principal Thomas gets annoyed with all the whistling and catcalls, and hustles Ms. Schaeffer away from the podium.

Then Mrs. Lane, who runs the drama club, steps up to the mike and says she has a special announcement.

"We have something pretty special lined up for the school musical next semester," she says, beaming at us. "Or should I say, some*one* pretty special. Nick Smart is a former Cumberland High student who's now a theater director on Broadway."

"See?" whispers Emily, who's sitting next to me

on the bleachers. "Some people *do* make it out of Cumberland alive."

"In fact, he was the youngest-ever director to win a Tony in the musical theater category!" Mrs. Lane looks so happy, I think she's going to cry. "Can you believe he's one of our own?"

"Go, Lobsters!" shouts some guy up the back, which makes everyone laugh except for Principal Thomas. He gets up and starts prowling the stage, on the hunt for the offender.

"Nick has offered to help make this year's musical the most successful and well attended in the history of the school," continues Mrs. Lane. "He is giving up his valuable time to work with me as codirector. He'll oversee a number of the rehearsals, and will even help to choose the students playing the principal roles."

Here she pauses for dramatic effect, and numerous people oblige her by letting out an exaggerated "Ooh." I bite my lip and glance over at Emily: she's doing the same thing.

"This means two things: First, we're going to have to hold auditions early this year to fit in with Nick's busy schedule. They'll take place immediately after Thanksgiving so we can have the whole cast in place before the holidays."

I nudge Emily and make a face; this isn't the greatest news. Normally, auditions are in the new year.

Thanksgiving is practically around the corner! It's one thing for me to promise I'll score a lead role for the first time, and another to be ready much sooner than usual.

"And secondly, Nick has made clear his choice of musical for our little production. As he's being so gracious and generous, giving up his extremely valuable time, I could hardly say no. So this year's musical will be . . ."

"The Pussycat Dolls!" someone shouts, and all his friends guffaw.

"I'm sorry to disappoint you," says Mrs. Lane, shaking her head. "But this year's musical will be *Grease!*"

"I knew it!" Emily exclaims, but nobody can hear her because they're all applauding and whistling. My head's in a whirl—not only are we doing one of my favorite musicals, but a real-life New York theater director is going to be working with us.

"Who told you?" I whisper to her as the noise dies down and Principal Thomas tells us we can all return to class.

"Nobody," she says, bouncing to her feet. "But isn't it weird that I start wearing my hair like Sandy, and now this?"

"So now you're going to try out for the lead?" I tease. We file along the bleachers toward the main doors of the gym, and I'm imagining myself in a big fifties skirt, skipping across the stage singing "Summer Nights."

14

"Yeah, like they'd give a redheaded dwarf the lead," retorts Emily. "You're going to be Sandy. You *have* to be. Why else would I suddenly get the urge to look like this? I'm telling you, it's a sign."

"If it were really a sign, wouldn't it be me with the Sandy hairstyle?"

"It would be if you were on the ball," she hisses. "But obviously you need me to have premonitions for you. Look—there's your chief competition. You're going to have to wipe her out this year, G."

I stumble on the stairs and have to grab Emily's shoulders to stop myself from a totally embarrassing fall. Down below us, bobbing with excitement, is the blond head of Terri Cooper, the girl who's had the lead in the last two musicals. Suddenly the image of me as Sandy evaporates, and I see myself in the chorus once again, stuck in the back row because I'm tall. Emily may think I'm destined to play Sandy, but it's going to take more than her new hairstyle to make that happen. It's going to take a miracle.

My family—the di Giovanni family—lives in an old, kind of ramshackle farmhouse, painted white with green shutters, near the top of a hill. My mother has been talking for years about painting the shutters a different color, but she can never decide *which* other color, so each year they just get a little more faded and chipped. Every so often she brings up the subject of paint color at dinner, and before long we're all arguing: I think they'd look really cool painted purple, my sister thinks they would be chic if they were black, my brother says we should rip off the shutters altogether and burn them, and my father says he doesn't care what color they are as long as he's not the one painting them.

Everyone in my family talks too much and argues all the time, especially at meals. The only time I can get my parents' attention is when they're getting dinner ready. They say they like to work as a team, but mostly they get in each other's way and squabble about how long things have to stay in the oven.

After school on Friday, I sit at the kitchen counter, telling them about Nick Smart and the auditions for the show. The steam from the stove has made my mother's curly hair even crazier than usual, and there's a smear of tomato sauce on her sleeve. She's only half listening, because my father is getting on her nerves by trying to stir something that doesn't need stirring.

"I wish I could ask Miss Sara's advice," I say. Miss Sara was my really amazing singing teacher at theater camp this summer. She used to be this big gospel star in the fifties, and had so many great stories about appearing onstage at the Apollo. She dressed in every color at once, and her singing voice was just unbelievable.

"Mike, don't keep taking the lid off that. Now, Grace, how about setting the table?"

I pull knives and forks out of the drawer and drift over to the table, still thinking about Miss Sara. She was really hard on us, in lots of ways, but I learned so much from her. Whenever she called me "Miss di-Gio-vanni" in that big, rumbling, almost operatic voice of hers, I wanted to jump to attention and stand up as straight as possible. She told me that if I wanted to be a performer, I had to stop slouching around like a stagehand and learn how to shine. That's what Miss Sara talked about a lot—learning how to shine, not being afraid of our own sparkle. It made perfect sense at the time, but I don't know how to explain it to anyone else without sounding too spacey.

I'm wandering around the table, dropping napkins next to each plate, when I stumble over something wobbly—Rascal's paw. The cutlery in my hand clatters to the ground, and the dog yelps, running into the kitchen, where he nearly knocks over my mother and whacks my dad in the butt with his tail.

"Grace!" my mother exclaims, exasperated. "All those years of ballet lessons and you're still falling over everything!"

"Hey!" shouts a voice from up on the landing. I spin around and see my sister, Sonia, leaning on the banister. She peers down at me through the reading glasses she'll only wear in the house. "Could you keep the noise down, Grace? I'm trying to work on my college admission essay!"

"Calm down, Sonia—it's only *August*," I tell her, but she's already stomping back to her room. She's planning a double major in college—French and economics—so she can become a translator at the UN or something. I think Sonia secretly wishes she already lived in France, or anywhere glamorous and European, which is why she acts like she's doing us a big favor by agreeing to speak English and eat American food.

"I wish your brother was working on *his* essay," grumbles my father, and starts complaining about how Tom lacks Sonia's discipline and focus. It's my cue to finish setting the table and escape upstairs. I know what Miss Sara would tell me: I have a whole lot of practicing to do if I want to "wipe out" the competition at the auditions.

Chapter Three

The drama club is agog about Nick Smart coming. There's no other word for it: everyone is AGOG. Even Mrs. Lane, who is normally sensible and levelheaded, and tells us that just because we're theatrical we don't have to be *hysterical*, is kind of agog herself.

"You don't know how lucky we are to have an actual Broadway director take an interest in our production," she gushes at our first after-school meeting of the semester. "This is the opportunity of a lifetime! We have to give it our all!"

Emily, sitting next to me in the circle of chairs, raises her eyebrows at me. "All or nothing, right, Mrs. Lane?" she asks.

"That's right, Emily—all or nothing," Mrs. Lane agrees, and Emily flashes me a smug, I-told-you-so smile.

It's the second week back, which means we've all had plenty of time to talk about this between classes and during lunch. Speculation is running wild about what the great Nick Smart is like: tall, dark, and handsome, by some accounts; more like the Hunchback of Notre Dame, according to others. Nobody has ever seen him, of course, though someone is rumored to have dug up his yearbook picture from ten years ago.

And surprise, surprise, we suddenly have a whole load of new members in the drama club. Last year only a dozen or so of the hard core showed up to meetings during the fall semester. At this year's first meeting, we have to keep adding to the circle of chairs. It seems that everyone at Cumberland High has discovered their dramatic potential—probably around the time Mrs. Lane said the magic word "Broadway." I mean, there are even boys here. In fact, with this many excited, overconfident, and not-too-talented people in the room, you'd think they were holding auditions for *American Idol*.

After the meeting, Emily has to rush off right away, because it's her cousin's bat mitzvah tonight. I stick around to help tidy up, scraping chairs back into position.

"How did you enjoy theater camp, Grace?" Mrs. Lane asks as she walks over to me. "We haven't had the chance to talk much about it yet."

"Oh, it was great," I tell her. "I learned so much. Miss Sara was such a wonderful teacher. . . ."

I stop myself, because all of a sudden I feel embarrassed. I don't want Mrs. Lane to think I'm dissing *her*.

"I knew you'd love her," says Mrs. Lane. "She's so inspirational."

"That's just what I told my parents!" I exclaim.

"She's especially good at helping young actors overcome stage fright," Mrs. Lane says, rummaging around in her bag and pulling out her glasses case. Someone calls her from the doorway, and she starts walking away. "That's why I recommended the camp for you. I thought you could really benefit from a strong dose of Miss Sara's medicine!"

Great. So Mrs. Lane thinks I'm a dodo who suffers from stage fright. Not that she's wrong—well, not one hundred percent wrong, anyway—but I guess she thought I was really in need of help. Last year when I auditioned for the school show, I just couldn't pull it together. My voice sounded okay, but my face was all flushed, I started hyperventilating, and my knees were shaking so hard they were practically knocking together. Emily said I did fine, but it just wasn't good enough. And it certainly wasn't my best. When I walked away, I felt like I'd let myself down.

The thing is, I have no problem at all once the show is under way. I love being onstage. I feel a surge of excitement when it's time to run on from the wings and take my place in a big number. I love looking out into the darkened auditorium to the blur of faces staring up at the stage, and singing and dancing my heart out. I love the costumes, even when they're made from cheap, itchy, sweaty fabric. I love the thick stage makeup that looks totally garish when you look at your face in the mirror, but seems perfectly natural once you're under the lights. And I really love the feeling of escape, of being someone else—even if that's just as a member of the chorus standing at the back of the stage. I'm still someone else, playing my part, helping to make the world of the show come alive.

But I'm not really happy about just being a member of the support staff; I dream of taking my place in the spotlight, of being the one to sing a solo, of getting swept up in the arms of the romantic hero. Deep down, I know I have what it takes—the talent, I guess, to play the lead. Talent's not enough, though, as Miss Sara told us day in and day out at camp. Talent's only half the picture—maybe not even half. You need determination as well, and persistence. You need to work hard and have a little luck come your way. And you need to be confident—not so confident that you're arrogant—but confident enough to know your own strengths and weaknesses, and still keep your cool.

"Think of it as a game of cards," Miss Sara told us in her rich, booming voice. "You're dealt a hand, a set of cards. In life, you have to play with the hand you're dealt. If you're a penguin, you can't make yourself a polar bear. If you're tall, you can't make yourself short. If you're tone-deaf, you can't turn yourself into an opera singer, no matter how hard you work and how much you want it."

I remember someone in our group making a snide comment—something about people who get the good cards always end up winning.

"Oh, no," said Miss Sara, holding up a hand like she was stopping traffic, all her bracelets jangling down to her elbow. "The winner is most certainly *not* the person who is dealt the best cards. The winner is the person who makes the most of the cards he or she has. Having talent is a wonderful thing, but remember, you need more than talent, much more. Like a card player, you have to take risks. You don't just sit there crossing your fingers and hoping everyone else has a worse hand than you. You have to make things happen for *yourself*."

I'm so preoccupied thinking about Miss Sara, that the sound of Mrs. Lane's voice behind me is startling— I've forgotten I'm back at school, helping to stack chairs in the drama room.

"Grace," says Mrs. Lane. "I know there's going to be a lot of interest in the show this year because of Nick Smart, and I know this is a busy time for you right now, but I wanted to tell you, I'm counting on you to take part. I need some of my old hands to help with the less experienced ones."

"Sure, Mrs. Lane," I say, trying to sound enthusiastic. She makes it sound like I'm a babysitter rather than a potential star: good old Grace, always reliable, there in the back row as usual, being a trooper. I'm only sixteen and already I'm an "old hand." Just what I wanted!

"And you'll be trying out for the role of Sandy, of course," says Mrs. Lane, and it's not a question. She's *telling* me. I'm so taken aback that I look around to see if she's talking to someone else.

"Well, yeah," I hear myself say. "Yes, I am. Well, that's what I was thinking, kind of, anyway."

Miss Sara would kill me for sounding so wishy-washy. Emily and I have watched *Grease* on DVD maybe two hundred times, and my mom took us to see the show when it was revived on Broadway a couple of years ago. I've listened to the cast recording over and over in the little CD player in my bedroom, acting out every number. I want to scream at Mrs. Lane and tell her that I AM SANDY, or I will be, anyway, by the time auditions roll around.

"I'll look forward to it," says Mrs. Lane, distracted once again by someone else wanting to talk to her—a boy called Jaco, who's never been to a drama club meeting in his life, but promises that his uncle can supply all the black leather jackets we need at cost. As long as Jaco gets a part, of course. Preferably a lead.

Let the craziness begin.

Outside in the school parking lot, only a few cars remain. I have to wait for Tom, who's still finishing up hockey practice. The three of us share a car—it's a dingy old Ford Escort, known as the Wagon—but there's a strict pecking order. Sonia has first dibs, because she was born five minutes before Tom. I'm at the bottom of the heap, of course. Practically the only time I actually get to drive the Wagon is when everyone else is asleep.

Sonia got a ride home today with one of her friends, but Tom and I finish up at around the same time on Thursdays. My father may say he's lazy, but Tom's really overactive, in my opinion: in the fall he plays hockey, and in the spring he runs track. Usually, if I get out of drama club before he's through with practice, I unlock the car and sit in the front seat and listen to the radio until he arrives. But today it's still warm out, and I'm bubbling over after the conversation with Mrs. Lane. *You'll be trying out for the role of Sandy, of course.* Of course! It's just not possible to sit still—I'm too busy imagining myself onstage, dressed in a puffy fifties skirt and skipping around a picnic table. There's nobody around, so I dump my bag inside the car and then take a few tentative dance steps. At summer camp, we learned a number that went: one, two, three and twirl, so off I go, arms outstretched, dancing around the car—one, two, three and twirl; one, two, three and twirl. Pirouetting was my favorite thing in ballet, though I'm not doing it correctly now. I should be focusing on the same spot every time I turn, but instead I close my eyes. Emily's right: it has to be all or nothing. I've been too cautious in the past, too worried about what other people thought of me. When these auditions come around, I have to be much more relaxed and confident than last year. I have to be ready to . . . *whack!*

"Ow," says a boy's voice, and I know, even before I open my eyes, that it isn't Tom.

"Sorry," I say, my vision still blurry. I'm staggering a little, too. This is why you're not supposed to close your eyes while whirling around in tight circles.

"Aren't you Tom di Giovanni's little sister?"

"Yes," I mumble, wishing my head would stop spinning. The guy I'm talking to is tall and has brown hair, but that's about all I can make out right now.

"I'm Hunter, by the way," he says. I squint at the rest of him—he's wearing a tight black T-shirt and dark jeans—and try to pull myself together, which isn't easy when the parking lot is still spinning. "Hunter Wells."

26

"Grace," I say, and notice that he's holding out his hand, waiting for me to shake it. I reach out just as he lets his hand fall by his side. Great—so now it looks like I'm trying to grab him. I know exactly what Audrey would do if she were here watching over me. She would bury her face in her hands in despair over my lack of social skills.

"So is this some weird ritual you're performing?" Hunter asks, his mouth twisting into a sardonic smile. "Putting a curse on Tom's car because he's late driving you home?"

"Something like that." What else can I say: that I was imagining I was Sandy from *Grease*, playacting like a little girl? This is Hunter Wells, after all. Everyone at school knows his name. I mean *everyone*. He's a senior, he's good looking, and he's our star quarterback. That all adds up to one thing: total A-list. Tom is in a couple of his classes, but how does Hunter Wells even know Tom has a little sister?

"I just saw him in the locker room," says Hunter, shouldering his gym bag. "He shouldn't be much longer."

"Great. Good. That's fine," I say, trying to sound nonchalant but saying way too much, as usual. I've only seen Hunter up close a couple of times, walking past him in the corridor between classes, because we move in completely different orbits. But now I notice that he

27

has the most intense blue eyes, bright and sparkling, like the lake up at summer camp.

"Does he give you a ride home every day?" asks Hunter. I can't believe Hunter Wells is actually standing around trying to make conversation with me. Emily will never believe this, not in a million years.

"Most days," I say. *Come on, Grace—think of something intelligent to say! Something witty and urbane, so he knows you're not some goofy kid sister who spends her afternoons skipping around cars.* Nope—I got nothing.

"It's a long time for you to wait around today, isn't it?" Hunter is so solicitous—he's much nicer than I expected. You would think that Cumberland High's best-ever quarterback—as Tom told us one night at dinner—would be snooty and arrogant.

"Oh, it's okay. I have drama club on Thursdays." At last I can speak in actual sentences.

"Drama club? That's cool," he says, his eyes twinkling, and my heart sinks. Drama club is so *not* cool. Whoever stars in the school musical has, like, fifteen minutes of fame while the show is on, but for most of the year, to most of the school, we're just theater geeks. "So have you met this big-time New York director yet?"

I shake my head. "He's not coming until auditions—after Thanksgiving."

"You better watch out for him," says Hunter, fishing

car keys out of his pocket. "He might try to lure you away to Broadway."

"Hope so," I shoot back, smiling. Tom appears on the other side of the parking lot, ambling along like he has all the time in the world. Hunter follows my gaze and raises a hand to wave at my brother. Then he unlocks the door of the black Honda Civic parked a space away from our car and slings his gym bag into the front seat. It looks like he's about to climb in as well, but he hesitates and turns around.

"One question," he says with a mock-serious frown. "When I walked up just now, and you were . . . you know, spinning around. Was that some kind of dance? Were you rehearsing some moves for the show?"

"No, not at all," I lie, but my cheeks are sizzling and I'm sure my blush is giving me away. "I was just, you know—in the moment!"

"In the moment? I like it." Hunter raises his eyebrows and gives me a broad smile. He has really good teeth. I know about these things: my father has a habit of pointing out good and bad teeth, usually in an embarrassing loud voice, whenever we're out in public. "See you around, Grace."

"Yeah, see you," I say, watching him get into his car. My face is so hot it feels sunburned. Tom finally drags up, looking at me suspiciously.

"What did *he* want?" he says, jerking his head in the

29

direction of Hunter's car, now making its way out of the lot.

"He was commiserating with me," I say. Now that Hunter's gone, I can talk like an intelligent person again. "He was worried that I was going to freeze to death or die of boredom standing out here waiting for you."

Tom rolls his eyes.

"Hitting on you, more like," he says. "You gotta watch out for guys like that, Grace."

"Guys like what?"

"Just get in the car," he says gruffly, and I can tell he's not joking. So I get in, smiling to myself, my head buzzing with all the year's possibilities.

Chapter Four

"Tell me again *exactly*," says Emily, leaning back against my locker, clutching her biology folder to her chest. It's the next day, and I'm filling Emily in on my encounter with Hunter Wells in the school parking lot.

"All he said was, 'See you around.' It's no big deal, Em."

"Are you kidding me? He totally initiated the conversation."

"He probably wouldn't have said a word if I hadn't hit him in the head or the shoulder or something."

"But he started talking and he kept talking—that's the main thing. And he asked you a ton of questions."

"Hardly!" Emily is way too carried away: I have to bring her down to earth before she starts levitating down the hallway. "Like I told you, it's no big deal."

"This is a total big deal, and you know it. Hunter Wells is not only a hunk, he's the A-team of the A-list. And he knew who you were, right?"

"He knew I was Tom's little sister. It's not like he had to hire a private detective for that. Come on, we're going to be late for class."

"Okay, okay," she sighs. Kids are swarming around us, thronging the hallway, and Emily moves away from my locker so I can pull my books out.

"I mean, 'See you around' doesn't mean anything," I tell her, slamming the door shut and turning around. Emily says nothing: she just stares all wide-eyed at me, as though she's just been struck by lightning.

"Hey, Grace," says a boy's voice, and that's when I see Hunter standing a few feet away from Emily. I hope he couldn't hear what I was saying.

"Hey," I say, and my voice comes out all squeaky. Emily was right when she called Hunter a hunk. He's wearing a black Lacoste polo shirt today, and it makes his eyes look even more blue.

"I wanted to ask if you're coming to Chris Valera's party tomorrow night," he says.

"Oh . . . well, you know. Maybe. Probably not." I don't know what to say, because of course I haven't been invited. Chris Valera lives in a house on the waterfront with its own jetty. It would take an ordinary human at least an hour a day to achieve Chris's look of studied casual: hair ruffled, collar turned up, everything just so. Sonia used to sit next to him in her economics class, but she said she had to swap seats with another girl—the smell of his cologne was giving her an allergic reaction. When Emily heard that story, she said she would have to be hospitalized with a head-to-toe rash to give up that seat.

"Well, you should try to make it," Hunter tells me.

"Yeah, I guess," I say, flushing hot again. I can just imagine ringing the bell and Chris Valera opening the front door. He would probably think I was delivering pizza.

"See you there," he says, flashing me a big smile as he walks toward a group of his buddies. Emily pulls me away in the other direction, because it's clear I'm not really capable of coherent thought or action right now, and marches me toward class.

"G, you *have* to go to that party," she murmurs, pushing me through the door.

"We haven't been invited!" I flop into my seat.

"Dude," she hisses. "Weren't you listening? You just were."

At lunch, sitting in our usual secluded spot at a table in the corner, Emily lectures me about my responsibilities to Our Junior Year. There's no way she can come to the party even if we both had official invitations; her parents are dragging her off to a family reunion in Pennsylvania this weekend.

"That doesn't mean you should suffer as well," she says, waving a spoonful of yogurt at me. "You should go, and if anyone asks you what you're doing there, just say Hunter Wells invited you."

It's easy for Emily to talk a big game. She's not going to be the one slinking through a party full of too-cool strangers, hoping that Mr. Popularity remembers who she is before the host humiliates her with a public confrontation and speedy eviction.

"Hey, Grace!" Terri Cooper stands over our table, manicured fingers gripping her lunch tray, though I'm pretty sure she doesn't intend to join us. "So, I'm guessing you're going to try out for the musical again this year?"

I nod, and she rolls her eyes.

"You and everyone else in the school," she sighs. "You know, it's going to be totally competitive this year."

"I guess so," I say, and it comes out really brusque. Something about Terri makes me feel mean inside.

"I was thinking," she says, flicking her long blond ponytail from one shoulder to the other. "Maybe you're ready to go for a bigger role this year—one of the Pink Ladies, maybe, or the cheerleader character, the one who's kind of nerdy. You could handle a few lines, I'm sure."

Emily pretends to choke on her yogurt, and I grimace at Terri.

"As long as you don't, you know, mess up at the

audition," she continues. "You know what you're like under pressure. And with an actual Broadway director there, well . . ." She gives me a fake sympathetic shrug.

"Thanks for your concern, Terri," I say. She's not the only one who can play fake. "I'll try and hold it together this time."

Terri sniffs to signal the end of the conversation and sashays off in search of an A-list table. Emily narrows her eyes.

"I don't know why you're so nice to her," she growls.

"I wasn't nice! I was being sarcastic."

"She doesn't get sarcasm," says Emily, scraping her yogurt container clean with ferocious precision. "All Terri gets are roles she doesn't deserve. Well, her luck is about to change, and I think she knows it—hence the royal visit just now. Have you decided on your audition piece yet?"

"Not yet." I shake my head.

"I just thought of something!" Emily's face brightens. "Terri will go nuts when she sees you at the party tomorrow night! She may even become mentally unbalanced. God, I wish I weren't going away this weekend."

I don't want to tell her that I'm still undecided about going to the party. Showing up, only to find a hostile Terri Cooper waiting for me is not my idea of fun. Emily would probably give me a big lecture about being wishy-washy, and not being committed to our all-or-nothing pledge. All I know is that it's easier to be brave when there are two of us sitting at a lunch table together, or two of us walking into a party together. One of me, all by myself? If this is what "all or nothing" means, "nothing" would be a whole lot easier.

At home, everyone's crazy with college applications. When I say everyone, I don't just mean Sonia and Tom. My parents are obsessed. We have college brochures stacked on every available surface—kitchen counter, coffee table, my mother's bedside table. Every night at dinner there's some big discussion about choices and scholarships and programs. For the first month it was interesting. Now I just zone out. I have plenty to obsess about in my own life without getting bogged down in all this a year early.

Sonia has narrowed her picks to five, and she's happy to discuss their relative merits and shortcomings all evening long. Sometimes she gets so carried away, her dinner gets cold and she has to get up and reheat it in the microwave. But Tom is still plowing through brochures and keeping his options open. That's what he tells our parents, anyway. I think he doesn't want to make a decision. Maybe he doesn't even want to go to college. In our family, that's total heresy. My parents have been saving so we could all go to college since we were babies, and my father has been giving his "education is the key to a happy and fulfilled life" speech for as long as I can remember.

It's not like Tom is a bad student or anything, but he's never been as focused on his future as Sonia. He's always been kind of happy-go-lucky, content to live for today. So maybe all this planning and deciding just goes against his nature. Of course, this kind of procrastination drives my parents crazy. It seems like every evening there's an argument waiting to happen.

That Friday, the night before The Party I Must Attend—according to Emily—everything erupts at dinner. My father is yakking on about which colleges my brother should consider, when suddenly Tom just explodes.

"Stop telling me what to do!" he says, his fork clanging to the floor. "I'm sick of talking about this every night!"

"You're sick of it? What do you think we are—happy that our son can't be bothered to plan his future?"

"Now, Mike," says my mother, trying to make peace as usual. "I'm sure Tom is thinking about this. He's just not ready to discuss it, that's all."

"Actually, Ma, I'm *not* thinking about it," Tom says defiantly. He can be a total hothead sometimes, just like my father. That's why they clash so much— they're two of a kind. "All I'm thinking about right now is whether the Patriots are going to win another Super Bowl."

"See what I'm talking about?" demands my father, and my mother shakes her head in despair.

"He's joking," says Sonia, her mouth full of salad.

"No, I'm not," Tom insists. "Just lay off, okay? Everyone. I'll start thinking about college when I'm good and ready, not when you tell me I have to."

"You want to work in construction forever?" says my father. He's really angry now. "Is that it? You liked it so much this summer, you want to spend the rest of your life hammering nails?"

"And what's wrong with that?" Tom says. "How is that any worse than picking at people's teeth for a living?"

"I'll tell you why it's worse—picking at people's teeth, as you call it, has paid for this house, the car you drive, the clothes you wear—try raising a family on a laborer's wages and you'll see why it's worse!"

"Maybe I don't care about money the way you do."

"Have we raised an idiot?" my father demands of my mother. This argument goes on for what feels like an eternity, until my father throws his napkin down in disgust and marches out to the garage, and Tom storms out of the house. Sonia shakes her head and wanders off to the living room, probably to calm herself down by rereading her favorite college brochures. My mother and I are left with the wreckage of the dinner table to deal with.

It's Tom's turn to help, according to the roster stuck on the fridge, but it's probably best that he's not around. He couldn't really be trusted around so many breakable objects right now. My mother and I clear the table, and she steps out into the yard to shake out the tablecloth. When she comes back in, I'm humming one of the songs I'm considering for my audition—it's called "Since I Don't Have You." My mother starts humming along.

"How do you know that song?" I ask, waiting while she rinses off the water glasses before I load them into the dishwasher.

"It's an old standard," she says. "Not to mention you've been playing it ten times every night for the past week."

"Sorry," I say. "I'm trying to decide what to sing at the audition for the school musical."

"You'd make a nice job of that," she says, smiling at me. She hands me a stack of plates to go into the dishwasher, and I decide to grab the moment.

"Ma, is it okay if I go to a party tomorrow night?"

"Whose party?" she says. This is always the first question my mother asks. An invitation in our house means an interrogation: who, where, when, and why.

"This kid at school," I say too quickly. "His name is Chris Valera."

"Valera . . . Valera," my mother wonders aloud.

"That name seems familiar. Don't we have a new librarian called April Valera?"

"I don't know," I mumble, jabbing a handful of forks into the dishwasher. Somehow I doubt that Chris Valera's mom works in the library.

"That's April Valentine, Ma," Sonia says, walking over to the counter from the living room. I thought she'd gone upstairs already. "The only Valera I know is the rich kid in my economics class. He's a total brat. He says he has to take economics so he'll know how to manage his trust fund. Can you believe that?"

Thanks a bunch, Sonia. I hope she drifts back to her college brochures before revealing any more incriminating evidence.

"And is this the Chris Valera who's having the party?" my mother asks. I don't need to turn around to know she's frowning. "This boy in Sonia's class? He's a senior?"

"Oh, Chris Valera has parties all the time." Sonia settles herself onto a stool and starts flicking through the pages of a magazine. "His parents have a place down by the water, and they go off on their yacht every second weekend. He does whatever he wants when they're away."

I'm willing Sonia to shut up, but she's completely oblivious. Why didn't I wait until tomorrow to ask my mother? Why did I have to blurt it out now while Miss

Killjoy is hanging around, providing all the worst kind of inside information?

"Grace wants to go to a party at his house tomorrow," my mother tells her, and Sonia snorts, looking up at me with an amused and incredulous expression.

"Who doesn't?" she asks. "Don't tell me you've been invited to one of Chris Valera's parties, Gracie."

"I have," I tell her. I know I sound defensive, but there's something about her tone that really grates on me—like she can't believe that *anyone* would want to hang out with me.

"How do you know Chris Valera?" Sonia closes her magazine.

"I . . . well, I don't know him directly," I admit. I guess I could say he's in the drama club or something, but Sonia would never believe that. "I was invited by a good friend of his."

"Who?" Sonia wrinkles her nose. Who needs parents when you have a detective for an older sister? I wish she would mind her own business.

"Hunter Wells," I mutter, and Sonia hoots with laughter.

"You know Hunter Wells," she says. "Now I've heard everything."

"Grace," says my mother, hanging a dishcloth on a hook and not noticing when it drops to the floor. "I don't think this party is suitable at all. This boy is a

41

senior and he sounds very wild. And you admit he doesn't even know you! Now, I don't know who this Hunter Wilson is—"

"Hunter Wells," chimes in Sonia. "He's a senior, too. He plays basketball or something, and all the idiot girls at school fawn over him."

"He plays football," I correct her, scowling.

"Whatever," says my mother, raising her hand. "Grace, you're too young to be going to unsupervised parties with seniors, especially if Sonia and Tom aren't invited. . . ."

"But I'm going to be a senior *next year!*" I protest. Sometimes I think my family sees me as a little girl, still in elementary school—little Gracie, who needs to be protected from the big, bad world.

"Then you can go to senior parties next year," says my mother. "Really, Grace, that's the end of it. I don't want to discuss this anymore."

"This is so unfair!" I say, slamming the door of the dishwasher. "Why do you believe everything Sonia says? She's just jealous because she wasn't invited."

"Doesn't sound like you were either," Sonia taunts, and I poke my tongue out at her. "Oh, that's real mature, Grace. No wonder seniors like *Hunter Wells* want to hang out with you."

"That's enough, both of you," says my mother. "We've had too many arguments in this house tonight, all right?"

I march out of the kitchen and up the stairs to my room, too furious to even look at Sonia. Thanks to her, I'll be sitting at home tomorrow night while Hunter spends the evening talking to other girls—the ones who fawn all over him, according to Sonia—and forgetting he ever met me. I press PLAY on the *Grease* CD and turn up the volume as loud as I dare. If Sonia thinks I'm going to use those headphones ever again, she's totally mistaken.

Chapter Five

All Saturday I'm still fuming. It's so unfair that I'm forbidden to go to the party just because Sonia does a character assassination on Chris Valera and my mother freaks out. I want to tell them that I don't *care* about Chris; it's Hunter I want to see. He made a point of telling me about the party, and I'm sure he'd talk to me again if I turned up. This was my big chance to spend time with him, to get to know him better, and now I've blown it.

Of course, I can't talk about Hunter with anyone in my family. The idea of mentioning a crush to my parents makes me want to crawl into the closet and lock the door. Sonia and Tom should have broken ground for me, but neither of them have, really. When Sonia goes out, it's always with a group of her brainiac friends, either to some cultural event or something goofy, like bowling. Tom goes out on dates from time to time, but he's never had a serious girlfriend. I wish I could talk to him about all this, but he's acted so mean and suspicious since the day I met Hunter, there's really no point. He seems almost uncomfortable around me right now, which is weird.

Emily has already left for her family reunion, so I send her a few plaintive text messages, hoping she'll reply with some words of sympathy. It's the middle of the afternoon before I hear back from her—just a brief "That sux!!!" She's right: it totally sucks. Yesterday, when I was thinking about going to the party, I wasn't sure if I would have the nerve to show up. Now that I know I'm not allowed to go, I'm absolutely desperate to attend. I lie on my bed, squeezing Oscar tight, imagining myself walking into the party. I'd cruise through the crowded rooms, ignoring any stares or comments, until I found Hunter. Not that I'd just walk up to him or anything—I'd need to play it cool. I could just hang out for a while somewhere close by until he noticed me and came over. Then we'd talk and laugh and . . . well, this part gets all blurry and vague, but I'm sure I'd make a good impression on him. I'd speak in whole sentences and make clever jokes, throw my head back and toss my hair, and act all animated and intelligent. Then I'd leave, suddenly and dramatically, just like Cinderella. He'd be despondent for the rest of the evening. Next week at school he wouldn't be able to rest until he tracked me down and begged me to go out with him, and I'd—

"Grace?" My mother taps on the door and opens it just wide enough to poke her head through. "It's too nice a day to be stuck inside. Why don't you walk over to Emily's?"

"She's not home," I say, and I'm just about to explain how Emily is out of town this weekend, when a lie suddenly slides right out of my mouth. "She . . . she has to go out with her mom this afternoon. But I'm seeing her later. We're going to the movies."

"That's good," says my mom, smiling at me. "I don't like to see you moping around like this. Is Emily's mother going to pick you up, or do you want us to take you?"

"Oh, Tom's going to drop me off," I say. That's lie number two. I can't believe I'm just saying all this stuff. Here comes lie number three. "Emily's not getting back until dinnertime, so we can't go out until around eight."

"Well, if Tom doesn't mind running you girls around, that's fine with me." My mother closes the door, and I keep very still, holding my breath and listening to her pad off down the hallway. I cover my mouth. What possessed me to come out with that string of lies?

Before the afternoon is over, I've come up with an elaborate plan. I've never lied like this before to my

46

family—never. But I'm in too much of a panic to feel guilty, frantically calling Tom's cell phone to see if he can give me a ride, squirreling away the newspaper so I can check on showtimes at the Savoy, the old movie house downtown. I cross my fingers that there's no nerdy *Star Wars* marathon showing, or some Italian film festival, where you can only get in if you're over eighteen. I'm in luck; this month they're showing a series of Hitchcock films, and there's a screening of *The Birds* at 8:10. I'm not a big fan of scary movies, but tonight it's crucial that I'm within walking distance of Chris Valera's house.

So here's the plan: I figure the party won't get started much before nine, so after Tom drops me off, I'm going to buy a ticket and sit through the first hour of the movie. Then I'll walk as quickly as I can to Chris's place—I've checked directions online, and it should take me no more than ten minutes. I can only hang out at the party for forty minutes, because Tom's coming back to pick me up at 10:15. I'll tell him that Emily already got a ride home or something. He won't question me the way my parents would, especially right now. He has way too much on his mind after that argument with Dad last night. I'm lucky that it's his turn for the car and not Sonia's. Tom missed the whole party conversation last night, so he won't be suspicious at all about my wanting to go downtown.

All through dinner my heart is pounding. Now that everything is straight in my head, I start feeling kind of guilty about what I'm planning to do. I feel bad about lying to my mom. I know she's looking out for me, but she forgets that I'm sixteen now. It's not like I'm going to be out really late or anything. All I'm doing is dropping into a party, saying hi to a few people—well, one person in particular—and then meeting up with my brother. I'm not hurting anyone or causing any trouble. Luckily, my father isn't around to ask me his usual nosy questions about where I'm going and what movie I'm seeing. He went out this afternoon with some of his golf buddies to check out a new course somewhere in western Connecticut, and he won't be back until after dinner.

As soon as I finish clearing the table, I race upstairs to get ready. This is the tricky part: I can't go too crazy, because usually when I'm going to the movies all I do is sling on a jacket and race out the door. But even the weather seems to be helping me out. It feels like a brisk fall evening outside, so I put on my jeans and a new white turtleneck, then cover it up with my peacoat. I stuff a lipstick and mascara into the pocket, to apply in the Savoy restroom before I head out to the party, and bound downstairs when Tom calls my name. There's the usual confusion as we're about to leave—Sonia's friends arriving to pick her up, the dog going nuts, my father choosing just that minute to call, Tom getting annoyed because he can't find one of his sneakers—and my mother is too preoccupied with the dishes to even notice me jog out to the Wagon. Everything seems to be working out just as I planned.

When the movie starts, it's hard to concentrate because my stomach is turning somersaults of nervous excitement. I can't believe I'm actually going to this party. Actually, I don't know if I have the courage. I've spent so much of today plotting and scheming, I haven't had time to worry about what's going to happen when I walk up to Chris Valera's front door. What if Hunter isn't there and I have nobody to talk to? What if one of Sonia's friends is there and reports me to my sister? What if Chris Valera won't even let me in? This is a real day of firsts for me: not only have I never behaved in such a sneaky and underhanded way before, I've never been to a party where I wasn't really invited. A party full of seniors who don't even know I exist.

I forgot to wear my watch, so every few minutes I turn on my cell phone to check the time, which gets me plenty of annoyed stares from the old couple sitting farther along my row. When it's finally time to go, I head to the restroom to make myself presentable, but the face in the mirror looks pale and scared. My hand is unsteady when I put on my lipstick, so I apply

49

way too much and have to dab it off with a paper towel. I know Emily says we have to stop hanging out with geeks and chess-camp types, but I've never felt this nervous about going out somewhere before. I wish Emily were here to give me one of her pep talks, but she's been incommunicado for hours. She's probably being kissed to death by elderly aunts and weird cousins right now.

Outside, a cool wind blows off the harbor, so I burrow my hands in the pockets of my coat and walk as fast as I can to Chris's house. In this part of town, the houses are old and crammed together, some of them leaning to one side. Chris lives in a big place on Water Street, set back behind a wrought-iron fence and creaky gate. The house looks like one of the mansions built by the old sea captains who used to live in Cumberland in between voyages around the world. It's three stories high, with turrets at the top and stained-glass windows on either side of the front door. The yard is manicured and pristine—no dog toys or broken hoses anywhere in sight—and the entire house seems to be ablaze with lights. As I turn the corner and walk toward it, I can hear the muffled sounds of voices and music. I slow down until I'm almost dragging my feet along the sidewalk.

Because it's not the warmest of evenings, there aren't any kids hanging around in the front yard. I hesitate at the gate and then push it open. The front door looks like it's slightly ajar, which means I won't have the humiliation of knocking and getting turned away. Maybe I can just slip in and lurk in some corner unnoticed until I spot Hunter. Where is Emily when I need her most?

I climb the stairs up to the front door and then hesitate again. At home I felt so grown-up and sure of myself. Now I just feel like a frightened little girl on her first day of school. Maybe I should get out of here right now. These aren't my friends. I don't belong here.

Just when I'm about to turn on my heels and make a run for it, someone pulls the front door open. It's a boy I vaguely recognize from school—not Chris, I don't think, but probably one of his gang.

"Oh," he says, staring at me with his mouth open. "I thought you were Sally."

"Nope." I shake my head. "Not Sally."

"There she is," he says, craning his neck to see around me. The gate creaks again, and a group of kids hurry up the stairs and past me without a second glance. They leave the door open wide, but I'm still standing there, looking dopey. Inside there's a grand staircase winding up to the next floor, and a polished floor that's as shiny as a mirror. The music playing in another room is loud, and I can feel the bass vibrating through my shoes. Or maybe it's just my thudding heart. What am I doing standing here—too scared to go in, not decisive enough to leave?

More kids are arriving now, and some give me strange looks as they push past me to get in. All I have to do is take one little step over the threshold, straight after one of these groups so it looks like I'm arriving with them and not by myself, like a pathetic loser. I take a deep breath. All or nothing, that's what Emily said. I've told so many lies to get here—I *have* to go through with it.

A car pulls up outside, and I decide that this is it: I'm going to tag along with whoever it is, whether they like it or not. I peer down at the street, looking to see who's climbing out of the car, hoping it's not someone awful like Terri Cooper. And then I freeze. The car parked outside is a pale blue Cadillac, and nobody's getting out of it. The only person I can see is my father, sitting in the driver's seat and looking straight at me. Even though the car is parked beyond the Valera's fence, and the streetlights don't seem particularly bright, I can tell he's very angry. I hang my head and start walking down the steps.

"Grace!" Someone's calling my name from the front door. I swing around and see Hunter standing there, beaming at me. "Greg said he thought you were out here. Aren't you coming in?"

I shake my head. I don't trust myself to speak right now. I might burst into tears. It's bad enough getting hauled home by my father before I've even set foot inside the party, but I know I'd better get my butt over to the car pronto—otherwise he'll probably come storming out to get me.

"Are you okay?" Hunter asks, taking a step toward me, and I shake my head again, glancing down to the street. My father's still in the car, but somehow I don't think he's in the mood to be kept waiting.

"I have to go," I whisper.

"Why?" he asks, sounding surprised and kind of impatient. He reaches out a hand to touch the sleeve of my coat, and I feel like I'm crumbling inside. "Is that your father out there? Do you want me to go talk to him?"

"No!" I exclaim. Hunter looks kind of aggressive all of a sudden, like he's ready to start some sort of fight with my father. I can't imagine anything more embarrassing. "I'm sorry . . . I just . . . I have to go!"

I hurry down the steps and toward the gate. More people are arriving, and I want to get out of here as fast as possible, before the entire senior class arrives to witness my humiliation. I jump into the car and close the door quickly, too miserable to speak. I glance up at my father, but he keeps staring straight ahead out the window. I can't remember the last time he was this mad at me. We don't speak at all, and I don't look back to see if Hunter is still outside the house, watching us leave. But he—and my chance at hanging out with him—seems to have drifted away.

Chapter Six

I'm in big trouble. Every time my parents look at me, it's with gloomy despair, as though I've totally gone off the rails. I know I've disappointed them—that's what they keep saying over and over. It makes me feel really awful, because I can see how unhappy they are.

"We thought we could trust you, Grace," my mother says, her eyes red with tears. "We never thought we'd have to worry about you lying to us. I can't tell you how disappointed we are."

Now I feel like a complete selfish jerk. It really wasn't worth it—going to the party, I mean. Not when this is the result. It was a stupid thing to do, and all because I wanted to talk to a boy. I can't tell them that I just wanted to spend time with Hunter. They'd think I was just a silly girl with a crush on the star football player. I must have been a fool to think Hunter was really interested in me. Sure, he was nice enough to me when he found me cowering on the doorstep, too afraid to come inside, not to mention terrified of the ride home with my furious father. But that doesn't mean anything. What must he think now, after watching me scuttle away and clamber into my dad's car? Little Gracie, scared of everything. What a loser.

To make things worse, Tom got in trouble as well. At first my parents thought he had been in on the whole thing, and it took me ages to persuade them he knew nothing about my scheme. But they were still mad at him anyway. They said he should have realized something was up when I wanted to go to the Savoy instead of the mall; he should have asked why Emily didn't need a ride; he shouldn't have left me there alone. My father was the one who figured everything out. Emily's mother had come to his office on Friday to get an annual checkup and told him all about the family trip to Pennsylvania. When he got home from his golf trip on Saturday night, and my mother said I was out at the movies with Emily, he smelled a rat. It didn't take them long to work out where I'd gone. I suppose I should be grateful that I *didn't* make it into the party itself. If my father had come knocking at the door, demanding I leave at once, the humiliation would have been too much to bear.

At school, Emily gives me loads of sympathy, and even tells me she's in awe of my bravery.

"I don't know that I would have had the nerve, G," she says. "Hoodwinking my parents and my brother like that, and going to the party on my own."

"But you told me I should go!"

"I didn't think you would. An A-list party full of seniors? That's a big deal. And your brilliant plan was pretty brilliant, you know. If only my bigmouthed mother hadn't made a pre-reunion vanity call to your father's office, nobody would have known anything. I'm impressed."

"Well, my parents aren't too impressed. I'm grounded until the twelfth of never." I hadn't been grounded since I ran up a two hundred dollar bill on my cell phone the month after I got it—I hadn't realized calling Emily every day would cost so much money, even though she was on vacation in Puerto Rico at the time.

"They'll forgive you," says Emily, trying to reassure me. "And they'll still let you audition for the show, right?"

I stop dead in my tracks, forcing everyone else pouring through the hallways to navigate around me.

"I hadn't even thought about that!"

"They can't be angry with you for another two whole months . . . can they?"

Great. As if worrying about the auditions weren't bad enough, now I'm worried about actually being *allowed* to audition. This is like the party dilemma all over again—scared of being there, scared of missing it.

Just to make everything perfect, I begin to notice some kids in my class whispering and giggling when I pass by. Everyone's talking—well, not everyone, but enough people to make school uncomfortable. The word is out about Saturday night: Grace di Giovanni turned up at the party and got dragged home by her father before she even made it through the front door. That's one version of the story, anyway. Emily reports back with another version—that Chris Valera was furious with me for trying to gate-crash and had the police take me away. On the way home from school—Sonia and Tom up front in the Wagon, me stuck in the back as usual—I hear an even worse account.

"It's so embarrassing, Grace," complains Sonia, who's driving, so she can't turn around to glare at me. All she can do is throw me mean looks via the rearview mirror. "Someone asked me today if it's true that you were clinging to Hunter Wells, crying and screaming when Dad arrived to march you home."

Tom starts laughing. I'm glad someone can see the funny side.

"I heard that Gracie tried to kick down the Valera's front door," he says. "I had to tell them that she has the strength of a hamster. She couldn't kick down the door of a doll's house."

"Thanks a lot," I snap. "You guys should be defending me, not making me look like an even bigger idiot."

"Hey," says Tom, twisting around in his seat to make a face at me. "You don't need *us* to make you look like an idiot."

"I can't believe I have such a juvenile delinquent for a sister," says Sonia.

"I preferred her when she was just a theater geek," says Tom. "But maybe this is what happens when theater geeks start growing up—they become drama queens!"

Now they're both laughing, so I refuse to talk to either of them anymore. I fold my arms and stare out the window, wishing I didn't have to go to school this week. I'd much prefer to hide out in my room until all this blows over and everyone finds someone new to pick on. I particularly want to avoid Hunter. He must have told people I was standing outside the party and that my dad was waiting for me in the car. He probably thinks this is all one big joke.

I spend the rest of the week lying low with Emily, racing from class to class, eating our lunch in the drama room. Hunter is the last person I want to see right now. I've provided enough entertainment for him, and now I've learned my lesson. I'm going to take my mother's advice and keep away from seniors—especially boys—until next year.

I have a lot of studying to do right now, so being grounded just means I have no excuse not to get on with it. Some of my teachers seem to think this is junior year in college rather than high school, and I have a ton of assignments to complete. Most of my evenings and weekends are spent sitting at the desk in my bedroom working on my homework, or curled up in my chair by the window reading *Great Expectations*. The title couldn't be more appropriate right now—my whole life is one big mess of hopes and dreams, and maybe none of them will ever come true.

Our street is pretty quiet most nights, especially as fall kicks in and it starts getting dark earlier in the evening. But sometimes when I'm reading by the window, I get distracted by the booming stereo of a passing car, or the whir of a skateboard cruising down the sidewalk. And the weekend after the party fiasco, when I'm sitting in my chair around dusk, kind of half reading, half dozing, the sound of pounding footsteps coming down the hill makes me look up from my book. I stretch up so I can see out the window, and see a jogger with his hood up, making his way along the street. He seems to be slowing right outside our house.

Even more strange, now he's pausing to stare at our house while practically jogging on the spot. Then all of a sudden he looks up at the bedroom windows. I can't believe my eyes—it's Hunter, gazing straight up at me!

I do what any self-respecting girl who's having a panic attack would do: I duck. Actually, I fling myself onto the floor and crouch there, hunched like a frightened animal, with my heart trying to beat its way out of my chest. What is he doing here? Why is he looking up at my bedroom window? I hope he didn't see me, though that seems pretty unlikely. And I don't know why I should be the one embarrassed about staring at him—this is my house, after all. Hunter doesn't live around here, I'm sure. Tom would know, but there's no way I'm asking him; he'd tease me from now until next Easter about having a crush on Hunter. And I don't have a crush on Hunter, not anymore—not since he blabbed all my personal business around school and made a fool of me. He's probably just here to gather more information.

After what feels like hours, but is really only around five minutes, I pull myself together and decide to risk peeking over the windowsill again. There's no sign of Hunter anywhere. I didn't hear him leave, but that's not surprising—the sound of my own heavy breathing might have drowned out his footsteps. He was probably appalled by the mess in our front yard. It's an obstacle course of dog toys, patches of dead grass under the trees, a broken sprinkler strewn through a wilting flower bed, and stretching across the front path, the leaking hose that never—and I mean never—gets put away.

I grab my phone to call Emily, and then change my mind. So Hunter jogged past our house; he's a football player and this is a big season for him—the last before he goes off to college. He probably has to run for miles every night to keep in shape, and he's just varying his route. I need to quit acting like such a gushy girl and not freak out every time I see him.

But the next night, there he is again, bending and stretching on the sidewalk, looking up at my bedroom window. I manage not to embarrass myself further by gawking down at him. Instead, I do a quick sprint into Sonia's room and kneel on her bed. That way, I can observe him through her window without getting noticed.

"What are you doing, *mon enfant*?" she asks me as I dash in.

"Just looking at the tree outside for my, um, biology project," I tell her. Luckily, Sonia's too absorbed in the magnum opus she's typing to ask any more questions.

The second night I rush into her room, she just gives

a deep sigh. "Do you have to examine the tree at exactly the same time every day?" she asks, pulling off her glasses and rubbing her eyes.

"What? Oh, yeah. That's it." I peer down at Hunter and stifle a laugh. He looks kind of ridiculous jumping around.

"You're weird, Grace. You know that? You're a weird little girl."

"Don't I make your life more interesting?" I scoff.

"You'd make my life a lot happier if you just decided on a song," she says, but I can tell by the tone of her voice that she's not trying to be mean. "Why don't you go with 'Since I Don't Have You'? It's the right range for you. You'd make a good job of it."

"That's what Mom said," I tell her. Sometimes I forget that Sonia used to be in the drama club too. She used to say she was going to be an actress when she grew up, before she decided that being a translator would mean a more reliable income. When I look out the window again, Hunter has disappeared. Maybe I'm hallucinating all this. I slump down on Sonia's bed.

"I thought you had to examine the tree," she says, all sardonic. "It is *the tree* you're looking at out there—isn't it?"

"What else?" I snap, and scoot out of her room before she has time to ask any more questions.

* * *

On Wednesday, I'm downstairs peering out from behind the living room curtains when Hunter comes thudding along the sidewalk. On Thursday, I don't expect to see him at all, because he has later practice after school. But there he is, not long before dinnertime, running through our neighborhood in his blue sweats, slowing down as he passes our house. All these days of seeing him without being seen myself must have made me bold, because on Friday, I decide to take a different approach. I mean, either this whole running-past-our-house thing is a huge coincidence, or he's trying to get my attention. Why, I'm not sure exactly, but there's only one way to find out.

Somehow it's easy to be brave here, because it's my home turf, not the Wild West of the hallways at Cumberland High. So I take my book out to the porch and sit on the swing, reading as I wait for him to run by. Actually, I'm mostly pretending to read. It's too hard to concentrate on the words of Charles Dickens when your head is full of the words of Hunter Wells—or at least, what he might say if he sees me out here today. I try out various casual poses so I can look up in a completely natural and surprised way if he stops by. Needless to say, they all look unnatural and contrived. Tom arrives home and stares at me with a mystified look on his face.

"Are you rehearsing a death scene or something?" he asks.

"No! I'm just reading my book!"

"Well, you look like you've fainted or something," he says, wrenching open the front door. "Why is your arm hanging there like it's broken?"

I decide to ignore him, shuffling into a more upright position as soon as he's inside. Just at that moment, I see Hunter round the corner and jog up to our yard. I snatch up my book and pretend to be intent on it.

"Hey!" he calls, a little out of breath. "Grace!"

"Oh, hey," I say, as though I'm surprised to see him there but not particularly impressed. Just because I'm sitting down here waiting for him doesn't mean I want Hunter to *think* I'm sitting down here waiting for him. He ambles across the lawn toward me, and I raise my book like it's a shield.

"So, I was just running—as you can tell," he says, with a goofy grin. He's standing at the bottom of the steps, looking up, his blue eyes piercing through me.

"And I was just reading, as you can tell," I reply, trying to keep it all breezy and casual.

"Ah . . . your book's upside down," he points out. I close it quickly and grip it tightly to me. So much for my cover of coolness. I have to think of something to say, quick.

"I just finished a chapter," I say, knowing that this is

the lamest possible excuse for holding a book upside down. Hunter grins. His face is flushed with exercise, and he looks totally cute in his sweats.

"I haven't seen you around school much lately," he says. "And I was just passing by, you know, on my run, and I thought I'd just . . . stop and say hi. I feel bad about the party. I hope you didn't get into trouble."

"Oh, you know." I shrug. Now I feel suspicious again. "It's not your fault."

"Well, I was the one who told you about it," he says, looking down at the ground and then glancing up at me again. "And you didn't even get in the door. As soon as I saw you, you ran off like Cinderella."

"I know." I can feel my face getting hot. "I didn't want you to see my father's car turn into a pumpkin. It freaks some people out."

Hunter smiles at me, and there's something about his face—its openness, maybe—that makes it impossible for me to believe he was the one spreading all the stupid stories. If he thought I was such a loser, he wouldn't be here now.

"You didn't miss much," he tells me. "I went home not long after you. We're not supposed to go to parties during the season, and I was pretty tired after the game."

"I forgot that you would have played football that day," I say, and Hunter frowns, like he thinks I must be lying. Really, I'm so unaware of the whole sports side of school. The Blue Lobsters could be state champions and I wouldn't know.

"You should come and watch a game," he says. "We're playing at home tomorrow."

"Sure," I agree, and then I remember that I'm still grounded. "Oh, actually, I just remembered. I can't go out tomorrow."

"Oh." He looks really downcast. In fact, he looks like he's about to walk away. At first I don't want to tell him that I'm grounded—it sounds so childish. But I don't want Hunter to think I'm blowing him off either.

"I wish I could come. It's just that . . . I'm grounded. Maybe next week?" I say hopefully. Surely my parents don't want me moping around the house forever. Hunter smiles up at me, and I don't know where to look. Neither of us say anything. Then the front door bangs open, and Tom bursts out as though he's been hiding in there listening to our whole conversation.

"Hey," he says to Hunter, his voice very cool. He turns to me. "You better get inside now, Gracie. Dinner's nearly ready."

"Yeah, I should be going," says Hunter, his voice pretty cold as well. He pulls the hood of his sweatshirt up around his head. "See ya, Grace."

"See ya," I say. I'm annoyed with Tom. Why is he treating me like I'm a little kid, practically ordering me into the house? I stand on the porch watching Hunter sprint off up the hill. As soon as he's out of sight, Tom goes back inside without saying a word. I'm not sure what he's got against Hunter, and he obviously doesn't want to discuss it.

I need to call Emily the second dinner is over.

Chapter Seven

The auditions for *Grease* are still weeks away, but that doesn't mean anyone's forgotten about them. Terri Cooper and her Rockette-wannabe friends are practically rehearsing numbers in the hallways. She's started coming to school with a little scarf tied around her neck and a cardigan draped over her shoulders like she's already in costume. Mrs. Lane is still trying to counteract all the rumors about Nick Smart—especially the one that has him pegged as a midget with a glass eye—but I think she's about ready to give up.

"He'll be here soon enough," she told us in drama club after yet another barrage of questions. "If everyone spent less time worrying about Nick Smart and more time working on their acting skills, we might have a good show this year."

I'm loading books into my locker at the end of the day when Terri sidles up.

"Hey, Grace," she says with a crocodile smile. "How's it going?"

"Fine," I say warily. Terri must want something. She never just stops by for a friendly chat.

"So," she sighs, leaning against the adjacent locker. Her neckerchief is pink with black polka dots; it matches her big swirly skirt. The word on the streets is that her mother is paying a seamstress to come up with all this fifties-style garb. She's sure not getting it at the Cumberland Mall. "I've been thinking that you'd be perfect for a certain role in *Grease*."

"Really." It's not even a question. Somehow I know the "certain role" isn't going to be Sandy.

"Mmmhmm." She nods, chewing on a piece of gum. "I was thinking that you'd make a fantastic Frenchy— you know, the beauty school dropout? Don't take this the wrong way, but you know how Frenchy is kind of goofy and unsure of herself? It just makes me think of you for some reason. You should really consider rehearsing her big number for the auditions. You'd make a total splash, I'm sure."

A total belly flop, she means. And anyway, Frenchy doesn't even *have* a big number of her own, as I'm sure Terri is aware.

"Thanks for the advice," I tell her, cramming another book into my locker.

"Just thank me when you get the part!" she says, all

bright and breezy, before flouncing off to rejoin her posse. I lean into my locker, wishing I'd come right back at her with some cutting remark, like suggesting she try out for the part of the frumpy principal, but I don't want to sink to Terri's level. And deep down, I wonder if she's right. She's probably going to get the part of Sandy—it's a no-brainer—and I'll be lucky to get a minor role. Terri's a senior; she's a proven leading lady, and she looks the part. I'm just Grace—a too-tall, brown-haired chorus girl.

Someone taps me on the shoulder, and I spin around, frowning. This better not be Terri, back with more "good" advice.

"What?" I snap, right into the face of Hunter. He looks a combination of startled and amused. I wish I could crawl into my locker and hide. "Oh my God, I'm sorry! I thought you were . . . someone else."

"If someone's bothering you, I can go deal with him, if you like," he offers, a broad smile lighting up his face.

"*Her,*" I tell him, smiling back at him out of nervous embarrassment. "I mean, no, that won't be necessary. But thanks for offering."

"No problem," he says, and then he leans one shoulder against the neighboring locker. Neither of us say anything. This feels like the longest minute of my life. There must be something I could ask him, like how the football season is going, or how his classes are going, or one of those other meaningless questions that make a conversation flow.

"So," he says at last, and then pauses again. There are people pushing past us, locker doors clanging, kids shouting to each other up and down the hallway. But all the noise and motion is one big blur, because I'm holding my breath. "So, I was just wondering . . . if you're still, you know, grounded."

"Just for another week," I say, feeling my face prickle with heat—it's so mortifying to have to admit to this. I look down at the floor and notice the blue laces in Hunter's sneakers, the kind of laces all the Blue Lobsters wear.

"That's good—I mean, that sucks," he says. "But at least it's nearly over. And I was thinking that maybe, when . . . you know, you can, and if you want . . ."

Another pause. My stomach's doing somersaults and I'm fixated on the floor.

"We could go out sometime," Hunter blurts, talking in such a hurry that it sounds like one long word. I can't believe my ears. "Maybe the movies, or something. Whatever. Your call."

"Sure," I say. "A movie. That would be great."

My voice sounds calm. Audrey would be so proud! Hunter beams at me, and his smile looks like one of relief. It's strange to think he's almost as nervous as I am; he always seems so confident.

"Next Friday, maybe?" he asks.

"That sounds good."

"Okay—well, see you." And away he lopes, disappearing down the hallway as suddenly as he materialized just a few minutes ago. I feel like banging my locker door open and shut with excitement, but instead I just stand there frozen—and smiling.

"G!" It's Emily, scampering toward me. "What did he say? Tell me everything, word for word."

"Did you see him?" I ask stupidly. I'm still in a daze.

"Dude, I've been standing by the window for the last five minutes. I totally had your back. I was ready to hurl myself in front of anyone who tried to interrupt your conversation."

Good old Em. Life wouldn't be half as much fun if she weren't there to discuss everything in endless, obsessive detail.

Surprise, surprise: my family is not overjoyed about my date with Hunter. They still think I should be going out on playdates with other little girls. You'd think I'd told them I was going out with a mass murderer, or planning to elope to Vegas next Friday. Talking to my mother about it is like a fencing tournament—I have to parry every thrust.

"I don't know, Grace. You're still grounded right now."

"Until Sunday, you said. I'm talking about next Friday—a whole week away."

"And I was planning to take you over to your grandparents next Saturday morning. I don't want you all exhausted and bad tempered."

"I'm not going to be out late. Hunter has a game on Saturday."

"I just don't like the idea of you going out with someone we don't know."

"*Ma*, we're going to a movie at the mall. And Tom and Sonia both know Hunter. He goes to our school, remember?"

"That's another thing. I'm not sure about you going out with an older boy."

"He's only a year older than me! It's not like he's in college or anything. And this is just going to the movies—we're not getting married."

"Well, it's hard to trust you after you lied to us about going to that party."

This is my mother's trump card right now, and it's not an easy one to argue with. But I finally persuade her by agreeing to a ridiculously early curfew.

My father stomps around looking gloomy, as though I'm leaving home forever instead of going out for a couple of hours on a Friday night. Even worse, Sonia and Tom are acting all disapproving.

"I wouldn't have thought you were the jock type,"

Sonia sniffs, after some secret confab with my mother in the kitchen. "Watch—you'll be going to football games every weekend."

I kind of expected this from my sister—she's such a snob about athletes, mainly because they rule our school, and someone with a Blue Lobster letter jacket is always going to be cooler than someone on the debate team. But I didn't think Tom would have objections as well. I corner him in his room to tell him about my upcoming date—not that it's any of his business, and not because I'm a gushy girl, but because I want him to say good things about Hunter to our parents so they'll get off my back. Instead of agreeing in his usual cheerful, laid-back way, he scowls at me and shakes his head.

"Just because a guy asks you out doesn't mean you have to say yes," he tells me.

"I know!" I'm so offended by this. It's not Tom's usual teasing, either. He's really serious. "Do you think I'm so lame and desperate I'd go out with just any-one?"

Tom shrugs and then turns his back to me, unpack-ing stuff from his backpack and scattering it across his bed.

"Could you at least tell Mom and Dad that he's an okay person?" I ask, and he says nothing. This infuri-ates me. "What have you got against him, exactly? If there's something so terrible about Hunter, why don't you just come out and say it?"

He sighs, throwing a rolled T-shirt onto the bed. "Would you quit pestering me? I'm kind of busy."

"What's up with you?" I demand. Tom has never spoken to me like this before. Suddenly I've got two fathers, both equally gruff and annoyed with me.

"I've got a lot going on right now," he says, keeping his back to me. "So sorry if I can't get all excited about your date with some loser jock, okay?"

So much for my cool older brother. He's just as self-absorbed and dismissive as Sonia. I march back to my room and bang the door closed. At least Emily's excited for me. I wish, this one time, my family would give me a break.

In the week before our date, I only get a glimpse of Hunter now and then at school. Just when I'm getting anxious that he may have changed his mind, he turns up at my locker to make arrangements—he'll pick me up at my house at seven on Friday night.

I can barely eat my dinner that evening. Even water tastes bad. After I manage a few bites and help to clear the table in record time, I race up to my room to get ready. This means trying on every sweater I own; they all feel too hot, or too skimpy, or too voluminous, or too boring. When the doorbell rings, I'm still picking through the pile of discards on my bed, feeling incredibly flustered. I don't know why I'm acting so crazy—this isn't the first date I've ever been on. But somehow it feels different, like it's the first *real* date of my life. In the past, the guy ringing the doorbell has always been one of my group of friends, someone fun to hang out with but nothing serious. This is the first time I've ever felt these intense butterflies in my stomach, this insane agitation about how I look and what I'm going to say.

There's no time left for dithering, so I pull on my red sweater and take one last look at myself in the mirror before I scramble down the stairs. I can hear my father talking in his usual overloud voice to Hunter, probably grilling him about his driving record, or making some embarrassing comment about the straightness of his teeth. My mother is hovering as well, just inside the door, peering out at Hunter like he's a dangerous animal who's escaped from the zoo.

"Hey," I say, squeezing between them and trying to sound as casual and carefree as I can muster. Hunter seems to be holding up well under parental scrutiny. He looks shiny and scrubbed, his leather jacket falling open to reveal a pale blue shirt. I can't help checking to see if he's wearing blue laces in his sneakers—no, thank goodness. There's only so much Blue Lobster loyalty a girl can take. The expression on his face is serious, probably to show my parents how responsible he is.

"Now, make sure you have Grace home by eleven," says my father, clapping a hand on my shoulder so hard I almost wince.

"Or maybe it should be ten thirty," says my mother. Great! At this rate we'll have to leave the movie before it's over just to make it home on time.

"We get out not long after ten, so that shouldn't be a problem," Hunter tells them earnestly. Maybe he's having second thoughts about taking out a baby like me.

But when we finally escape their clutches and drive off to the mall, he's all smiling and friendly again.

"Sorry about my parents," I tell him. "They're kind of protective."

"You're the youngest, right?"

"Yeah. I thought the youngest was supposed to have it easy."

"I'm the oldest in my family," he says. "I always think my two brothers have it easier. There's just us and my mother. My father hasn't been around since I was a kid. So we all try and look after *her*, I guess."

I don't really know what to say, but Hunter starts talking about the movie we're going to see, and how he called ahead for tickets to make sure we get in. I want to ask him more about his family, yet I don't want to seem too nosy. But something about the tone of his voice makes me care about his personal life. It seems like he's a really honest and genuine person.

78

Because it's Friday night, the mall is packed, and I see a few kids I know from school in line to get tickets or buy popcorn. Two girls from my gym class stare at me with openmouthed curiosity when they notice who I'm with. Hunter gets our tickets from the machine, and then insists on buying us each a giant cola. I'm not at all thirsty, but I'm happy to have the prop. When we take our seats, there's still twenty minutes until the movies starts, so I can sip on my drink if there's a conversation lull.

We find two seats together near the back, and my stomach starts turning somersaults again. Our shoulders are brushing, and when Hunter leans forward to place his cup in the holder, his hand knocks against my right knee. My entire right side prickles with goose bumps. A group of guys down front wave at Hunter, and he raises a hand to acknowledge them.

"Do we know every single person in here?" he asks me in a low voice, wriggling down a little lower in his seat.

"They're following us," I joke, and then look over my shoulder to see who's sitting behind us. And that's when I see my brother sitting by himself in the next row up. Tom catches my eye and stuffs a handful of popcorn into his mouth. He doesn't even pretend to smile.

I scowl at him, and Hunter turns to see what I'm

looking at. He lets out a sort of wheezy laugh when he sees Tom.

"I guess your brother wants to keep an eye on you," he says, raising his eyebrows and giving me a conspiratorial grin. "You're lucky to have such a close family."

Yeah, right. I don't feel very lucky. I feel like I want to kill someone—preferably my uninvited chaperone, the one whose eagle eyes are drilling into the back of my head. At least the lights are going down, so Tom won't be able to see anything but the screen.

Chapter Eight

"So did he kiss you?"

This is Emily, of course. We're sitting together in the stands, watching the Blue Lobsters take on the Eastport Jaguars, the day after my movie date with Hunter. It's a sunny fall afternoon, but there's a hint of crispness in the breeze, so I have a scarf wound around my throat to protect it. I have to start getting serious about voice training again.

"Sort of," I tell her. "I mean, he walked me up to the porch and gave me a peck on the cheek."

"Not bad." Emily screws up her face as though she's deep in thought. "It could be worse."

"What do you mean?"

"He could have shaken your hand and sprinted back to the car. Hang on a sec." She scrambles to her feet, oblivious to the complaints from the people sitting behind us, and snaps a few shots of the players on the field before sitting down again. "Sheesh—you'd think there was something exciting going on down there. Calm down, people. It's just guys standing around drinking water."

"Why did you take the picture, then?"

"I'm trying to get a close-up of Hunter for you," she whispers, and I can't help laughing. Hunter is almost unrecognizable in his uniform and helmet; though—as Emily pointed out when we sat down—his butt looks pretty cute.

"So it was nice," I tell her, getting back to the topic of the kiss. "But he was probably rattled after seeing my stupid brother watching us like a hawk in the movie theater. Maybe he thought my father was going to spring out of the house the moment he heard our footsteps on the porch. He must think my family is so freakish."

"What is *up* with Tom?" Emily shakes her head.

"Just overprotective, like my parents," I say. "They all want me to stay the same, I guess."

"You know, when I saw you today," Emily confides, "wearing that scarf, I thought that maybe Hunter had given you hickeys all over your neck."

"Emily! As if!"

"Hang on a sec." Emily leaps to her feet, hoisting her camera up as two players tumble across the sideline. "Damn—missed it. Oh, well."

"I don't think you have any idea what you're

doing. Shouldn't we be sitting much closer?"

"Thanks very much for the vote of confidence," she says indignantly. "Actually, my job today is to take wide shots, if you must know. And speaking of jobs, I hope you're getting plenty of rehearsal time in. Word is that Nick Smart's going to be dropping by Cumberland High next week on a reconnaissance mission."

"How do you know these things?"

"Maybe I'm not floating around in my own little world like you, dreaming of boys. By the way, did he say anything about a second date?"

I nod, my face breaking into a wide smile.

"He says he's got some gift certificate for a seafood restaurant in Mystic. He asked me if I wanted to go next Saturday night."

"I knew it!" Emily declares. "I just knew these football players get bribes. We might have to expose this in the school newspaper."

"Relax, will you? He got it from his uncle—for his birthday. And by the way, you're missing a touchdown."

Emily can barely hear me, because everyone in the stands is going crazy. I jump to my feet to cheer the Lobsters, while she's still glued to her seat, fumbling with the camera.

Emily's right—not about the football player payola scandal, but about me being in a daze. Even though I'm getting through all my schoolwork without a problem, and going to drama club as usual, and studying in the evenings, just like Normal Grace would do, I don't feel "normal" at all. First of all, I'm practicing my audition number, "Since I Don't Have You," every single night, not to mention every time I take a shower. I could just about sing it in my sleep. And even though I hardly see Hunter at all at school, because we have different schedules and classes and friends, he's on my mind an awful lot, like a song you hear on the radio and can't get out of your head. Some days I don't know what makes me more nervous: the thought of auditioning for Nick Smart, or the thought of going out again with Hunter. Both give me butterflies in my stomach, but it's the thrill of excitement, not dread, that I'm feeling.

My parents agree to my going out to dinner on Saturday, but not before I've listened to a big lecture about the importance of driving safely, the importance of saying no to drinks, and the importance of arriving home no later than 11 P.M. in order to continue the ten-year process of earning back their trust. My father thinks that Hunter drove away just a tad too quickly the other night when we went to the movies, and now he's all antsy about Hunter being a secret speed demon. My first impulse is to say something sarcastic about getting Tom to follow us, but I hold my tongue. No point putting ideas in their heads.

Tom and I are barely on speaking terms right now. I hate it when he and Dad argue, but I hate it even more when he acts as Dad's henchman, turning up to spy on me. I'm glad he's not around when Hunter arrives on Saturday night to collect me.

My mother answers the door this time, and at least makes a pretense of being nice to Hunter, asking him in and not grilling him with *too* many questions. Hunter looks well scrubbed, and he smells nice, too. He chats with my mother about today's game while I pull on my coat and wrap my scarf around my neck.

"It's chilly out tonight, Grace," she says, and then turns to Hunter. "She has to protect her throat. The big auditions are coming up soon."

"Oh, yeah," he says, looking kind of perplexed. We haven't really talked much about my musical aspirations yet. My father emerges at this point to discuss the exact mileage to Mystic and the speed limits of every road en route, something he's spent the last hour looking up online. I like the way Hunter is really polite to my parents, though maybe this is because he senses how irrational and extreme they are: one wrong step and they'll never let me out of the house again.

It's one of those beautiful early fall nights, when you can smell wood smoke from chimneys, and the leaves are starting to turn a rich golden color.

"This is my favorite time of year," I tell him when we get in the car.

"Mine too," he says, grinning at me. "I was hoping we'd get to Mystic in time to see the sunset, but the nights are closing in pretty early already. And I promised your dad I'd do a steady thirty miles an hour the whole way."

"I'm sorry," I say, rolling my eyes. "My parents are . . . well, I don't know what they are. Crazy, I guess."

"They're just parents." Hunter shrugs. "You're lucky having two who look out for you."

There's a longing in his voice, and I remember what he said last week about his father leaving when he was a kid. However annoying my father is, I can't imagine growing up without him around.

"You must be pretty close to your mom," I say.

"Yeah," he says, checking over his shoulder before he turns onto the main road. "I don't see much of her at the moment, because she's working extra shifts at the hospital. But we've always gotten along well. It makes college stuff kind of complicated, though."

"How do you mean?"

"Well, I know it sounds sappy, but I don't want to move too far away. My brothers are still pretty young, and my mom's going to find it tough if I up and move out to California, say. But where I go to college isn't up to me, really. I'm trying to get a football scholarship, so it's up to the scouts. I'd like to go somewhere close, like Penn State. But it's not just about getting into a school—it's about being good enough to make the team."

"That must be a ton of pressure," I tell him. I think I have it bad, having to study hard and choose a college, but Hunter clearly has a lot more at stake.

"Yeah, I guess. And if I get a good offer from a school, I have to take it, no matter how far away it is. We can't afford it otherwise."

Now I really do feel like a little girl. I've never even thought about what "we" can afford, because I'm still in the mind-set of my parents being the big providers and me just taking. Hunter is way more mature and thoughtful than I am. And he's got a real soft side—not what you'd expect from a cocky A-lister who's the hometown football hero.

"I thought we'd take the coast road," Hunter says as we pass the highway entrance. "It'll take longer, but it's more scenic. You're not in any hurry, are you?"

I shake my head and smile at him. Right now, I'd like this evening to go on forever.

We eat dinner at the seafood place, which is on the harbor, and though it's too cold to eat outside, we can still see the boats and seagulls through the window next to our table. I manage to eat clam chowder without dropping any creamy globs down my sweater, though I don't think I've ever felt this self-conscious eating a meal before. Hunter chows down an enormous amount of food and apologizes for being so greedy—he's always this way after a game, he says.

It's easier to make conversation than I thought it would be, maybe because none of my family have snuck into the restaurant to spy on us, or maybe because it feels like we're a world away from school and Cumberland and everyone we know. Whatever my brother and sister think, Hunter's no dumb jock. He's pretty intense, actually. He tells me more about his mother and two little brothers, about working for his uncle's optical supply company for the past two summers in order to save enough to buy a car, about his favorite classes and teachers. And he asks me lots of questions, too, so I end up going on about theater camp, and talking a whole lot about Miss Sara and the things I learned from her. I mention the audition coming up.

"You'll ace it," he tells me, rummaging in his pocket for the gift certificate so he can pay the bill. "I have complete confidence in you."

"Thanks." I feel myself blushing at the compliment. "But I'm not as experienced as some of the other girls who'll be trying out. Some of them have had lead roles before, and I've just been in the chorus."

"That was then," he says, shrugging. "This is a whole new year. And you're a different person—you said so yourself."

"I guess," I say. "But I'm still nervous about it. Do you ever get nervous before games?"

"Yeah," he confesses. "It's part of the adrenaline rush—you have to use it to your own advantage. Sports aren't that different from what you're talking about. You're putting yourself out there in front of a big crowd, and you need to deliver a good performance. There's pressure, but it's exciting as well. You have to take the risk."

"It's the risk that frightens me, I guess."

"Really?" He looks surprised. "But you want to take the risk, right? You don't seem like the kind of person who would be happy always watching from the sidelines."

"I'm not," I say. "At least, I don't think I am."

"And there's always going to be someone with more experience than you. You have to focus on what you have, not what you're missing. Keep looking forward. Sorry if this sounds like preaching—Coach is always going on about this kind of stuff."

"He and Miss Sara have a lot in common," I tell him, and he smiles.

"Anyway, you have something about you that those other girls don't," he says, but then the waitress comes over to ask if we want anything else, and when she walks away I'm too shy to ask him what he meant.

After he pays the bill—refusing my offer to contribute to the tip—Hunter suggests we take a walk. We wander up along the harbor and across the bridge leading into town. It's dark now, but the sky is bright with stars. Moonlight makes the calm harbor waters sparkle, and the night feels so still we can hear the boats creaking against each other in their moorings.

We stop on the bridge to look out over the water, standing shoulder to shoulder as we lean against the railing. My heart is pounding so fast and so loud, I'm sure Hunter can hear it.

"I know it's kind of a long way off," he says, not looking at me, still staring out toward the sea. "But . . . well, I was wondering if you'd come with me to the end-of-season awards dinner. It's a pretty big deal. It's not until the first week of December, but I figure you might get booked up pretty quickly."

"I . . . I'd love to," I stammer, and we turn our faces to each other. Mine is red, I'm sure, flushed with nervousness and excitement. Hunter's is shining—it's the moonlight, maybe, or his smile, broad and happy. Then he leans toward me, and instinctively I turn my face up to meet his. Our lips touch, and then our noses, and the kiss feels warm and soft. When he gently pulls away, I'm short of breath, giddy with the sensation of it.

We stand together facing the water again, but now he has an arm around my waist, pulling me close. Neither of us says anything. Just being in the moment—right here, right now with Hunter—makes me indescribably happy.

Chapter Nine

Suddenly my life seems to be on fast-forward. October whirls by in a blur, and November is even more frantic. Not only am I going out with Hunter once a week—all our schedules and my parents will allow—but I have voice lessons, drama club, and an unreasonable amount of assignments and tests to work on. Any Saturday afternoon the Blue Lobsters have a home game, Emily and I are there, but I have to miss the homecoming game when my voice teacher switches lesson times on me. Hunter's disappointed, but he's also pretty distracted at the moment; college scouts are there every weekend, and some even drop by to practices, so it's make-or-break time for him.

The week before Thanksgiving, Nick Smart himself turns up at the school assembly to smile and wave and prove to us, once and for all, that he's not a goblin with a walking stick and blue hair. Actually, he looks pretty normal—neither tall nor short, with dark hair and the first hints of a receding hairline. He's wearing gold-rimmed aviator glasses, a tailored black jacket, and jeans. Emily, who has brought a pair of mini-binoculars to school in order to get a closer look, reports that his shoes need polishing and that there's a small stain—possibly coffee—on his shirt. The way Principal Thomas and Mrs. Lane are fawning all over him, you'd think he was a Kennedy or something. Nick Smart looks pretty pleased with himself, but I guess I'd be pleased too if I'd had his success on Broadway. Mrs. Lane introduces him and asks him to say a few words.

"Nothing changes around here, does it?" he says, adjusting the microphone on the podium and then running a hand through his slicked-back hair. "Still the same old Cumberland High, right?"

There's a little polite laughter from the bleachers, and then Nick Smart steps even closer to the microphone and lowers his voice.

"Well, I'm here," he says, and then pauses, looking around the gym, "to SHAKE THINGS UP!"

This gets a better reaction, especially from the peppy A-list girls, who are all programmed to squeal and get excited when someone even peppier than they are makes a speech.

"People," he continues, "this year's musical is going to put Cumberland High on the map, and I don't mean the map of Connecticut! Just because we're off-off-off

Broadway here doesn't mean we can't be ON, ON, ON!"

Ms. Schaeffer leaps to her feet and starts applauding. She loves this kind of thing. I look over to where Hunter is sitting—with all the other Blue Lobster players, as usual—and discover he's gazing up at me, a sardonic grin on his face. He winks at me when he catches my eye, and I'm sure he's going to have something to say about Nick Smart when I see him later today.

"Now, don't get too excited," says the man himself, holding up a hand to silence the crowd. "We've got a lot of work to do. But I wanted to drop by before you all head off for Thanksgiving break . . ."

"Head off?" whispers Emily. "What, does he think we all go skiing in Switzerland?"

". . . to tell you that auditions are coming up, and I want you to be ready. In fact, I want you to be ready to EXPLODE!"

Ms. Schaeffer obligingly explodes out of her chair again, jumping up and down with excitement. Principal Thomas shoots her a "Be cool" look, but she doesn't notice. Mrs. Lane beams at us all. She's not used to everyone showing this much enthusiasm about a school show.

"This year, only the very best will make the cut," says Nick Smart. "So spend the rest of this month getting ready to rock me. I don't care how many starring roles you've had in the past—this is a whole new ball game."

Emily nudges me.

"I want to see talent," Nick continues. "And I want to see heart. I want to find the rising stars of Cumberland High. I know you're out there, and you have less than a month to get ready. Don't disappoint me, okay?"

He waves to us all and then sits down. Mrs. Lane hurries over to the microphone.

"Just one reminder," she says. "Because of Nick's incredibly busy schedule, auditions have to take place on a Monday, when the Broadway theaters are closed. So we've tied him down to the first Monday in December. Got that? The first Monday in December. Girls in the morning, boys in the afternoon. Members of the drama club, you get precedence signing up for a time slot."

Everyone who's not in the drama club, i.e. ninety-eight percent of the school, starts booing. Principal Thomas gets so annoyed he barks "School dismissed!" into the microphone and then stalks off, leaving the teachers and their honored guest alone onstage.

Everyone around me is standing up and stretching, and I can hear at least one girl declare that she is completely and utterly in love with Nick Smart, but I'm preoccupied with flicking through my date book to mark down the day. When I find it, I scramble to my feet and elbow Emily so she'll put away her binoculars and pay attention to me.

"You should see the look on Terri Cooper's face," she whispers. "Sort of panicky and vacant at the same time. Maybe she knows that she doesn't have talent *or* heart. Just really blond hair."

"Em," I mutter. "Look!"

I flap my date book in her face and she squints in noncomprehension.

"Hunter's awards dinner," I hiss. "It's the first Sunday evening in December. The auditions take place the next day. Even worse—the next morning."

"It won't go really late, will it? The dinner, I mean. It's a school night for them, too."

"Only kind of—don't you remember from last year?" We file out of the gym and into the crowded hallway, and I pull Emily over to a quiet corner. "It's Blue Lobster something or other, when the team and the cheerleaders get to cruise in whenever they like. That's why we can have our auditions during the day instead of after school—classes are messed up already."

"I don't remember this Blue Lobster Day thing!" Emily protests.

"It's because we didn't know anyone remotely Blue Lobster-ish last year," I say.

"True, we weren't in the Blue Lobster cult," Emily

96

agrees. "Those were such innocent, simple times," she says, gazing up to the ceiling with mock reverence. "How I long for them."

"No, be serious! I don't want to jeopardize this audition. This is it, remember? The big thing you've been lecturing me about for months."

"I know." Emily nods. "And now your choice is Love or Art. It's romantic!"

"It sucks," I tell her.

"What do you think Audrey would do?" she asks, hugging her books to her chest and frowning.

"The Audrey in the movies would give up everything for love," I say. "But the real-life Audrey would probably go to bed early with a cup of tea and some Throat Coat."

"You know what we should do?" Emily's face brightens. "Let's race and find Mrs. Lane now, and sign you up for the last possible audition slot that morning. That way, you can stay out late with Hunter but still have time to recover the next day."

Emily is a genius. We scamper off down the hallway toward Mrs. Lane's classroom and the perfect solution to my problem.

But by the time we get there, we're already way too late. Every girl in the drama club is on the exact same brain wave, and all the late-morning slots are filled. Terri Cooper and her friends have a complete monopoly on anything after ten thirty, and I know there's no way any of them will agree to swap with me.

"I'm sorry, Grace. The best I can give you is nine thirty," says Mrs. Lane. "But that's not a problem, surely? Just pretend you've been booked to sing on the *Today* show and do what the professionals do—go to bed early on Sunday night, and you'll be fresh as a daisy."

"Or cooked," Emily groans after we leave the room.

"I'll just have to go home earlier than I planned, that's all," I say, trying to make the best of it. This is so crazy—I spent a good half hour every weekend pleading with my mother to let me stay out until midnight, and now I'm going to tell Hunter I have to be home by ten. Probably the dinner will be over by then, but there's a big party that everyone's invited to afterward.

"He'll understand," says Emily. "It's not like you're not going *at all,* or anything. You just won't be able to go to the glamorous after-party at some fabulous club or mansion. And Hunter will have to leave the biggest event of the year—maybe of his life—to take you home real early, possibly while everyone else is still eating their dessert. What's the big deal?"

"You're not cheering me up," I tell her, while hurrying toward my locker with my head down. Why does everything have to be so hard?

* * *

Even though I keep telling myself that Hunter is going to be fine about my self-imposed curfew on the night of his big awards dinner, I drag my feet about mentioning it to him. The Sunday afternoon after Nick Smart's visit, Hunter and I go for a walk through the park together, holding hands and scuffing through the crunchy golden leaves.

He's in such a good mood, I don't want to spoil things. And we won't be seeing each other much over Thanksgiving. His mother is on call at the hospital, and he has to be around for his brothers. Meanwhile, I'm being dragged off to my aunt's house in Massachusetts, for three days of loud TV, overeating, and family "discussions" that instantly descend into arguments and only stop when it's time for another huge feast.

But after we've been walking for a while, Hunter brings up the subject of the audition himself.

"You know, I've never heard you sing," he says, swinging my hand. "Maybe I should try sneaking in and sitting behind that Nick Smart guy."

"Sorry—no boys allowed until the afternoon."

"Doesn't matter. I'll be able to come to every performance when the show's on. No place to hide for the star. . . ."

"Very funny. I'll sing for you sometime, if you really want."

"Right now?"

"In the car. Maybe."

He drops my hand and wriggles his arm around my waist. "Either way, I'll still come to every show. That's the way it works, right? You're there for me on my big night, I'm there for you on yours."

I nod, looking down at the ground, and Hunter keeps talking, wondering aloud if he'll get MVP this season.

"I know it sounds kinda childish to want something like that," he says. "But it's a big deal, especially because it's my last year, and especially because it's *this* year."

This was the Blue Lobsters' best season ever, according to the banners Ms. Schaeffer's over-caffeinated sorority squad has been draping all around school. Hunter has even been interviewed by the local paper—the headline read "Lobster QB Headed for Big Ten?"—about all the college scouts who've been expressing interest. He's not bigheaded about any of this, but I know it's important to him. So when he talks about me being there for him, I feel utterly guilty. There's no point in putting it off any longer.

"I just . . . well, I just realized something about my audition," I falter. "It's the day after your awards dinner."

"Really? I thought they were happening right after

Thanksgiving." Hunter kicks through a pile of leaves and grins with pleasure like a little kid.

"Yeah, and the thing is . . ." Why is this so difficult to say? "The thing is, I have to sing pretty early. I mean, relatively speaking. So when the dinner's over, I need to go straight home. I won't be able to go to the party afterward."

"Really?" Hunter sounds disappointed, and when I glance up at him, he looks crestfallen. "Even for an hour or two?"

I shake my head.

"I really need to get a good night's sleep, and not wreck my voice." I try to explain to him about not being around smoke and loud music, but I can see he thinks I'm overreacting, especially when I say I'll need to leave by ten.

"The awards ceremony might not even be finished, Grace," he says, and for the first time I hear annoyance and impatience in his voice.

"I'll totally stay until you get your award," I say quickly.

"*If* I get it." He unclasps my waist. "Whatever. Even if I do win it, you'll be gone the next minute. I'll be the first-ever MVP to have his date walk out on him."

"Don't be like that," I plead. "You know how much I've been looking forward to it. These are special circumstances."

He shrugs, and we head back to the car, not speaking. When he drops me off at home, I lean over to kiss him on the cheek and he tries to flash me a smile, but it's forced, I can tell. Inside, I take off my coat and listen to his car screech away. My mother appears out of nowhere, clutching a big white shopping bag in her hand. It's from La Laine's, the fancy shop downtown.

"Grace, I know I shouldn't have done this, but . . . Oh, I can't wait to hear what you think." I'm guessing she's bought herself some new dress and wants to show it off, but I'm really not in the mood.

"Ma, can it wait until later? I've got a lot of stuff to do right now."

"I think you'll want to see this," she says, her face pink and happy. So I heave a big sigh and flop onto one of the lower stairs, trying not to look irritated. Can't she see I have other things on my mind right now?

"Okay—so you have to tell me if you don't like it, and I can take it back. It's just, I saw it yesterday and thought it would be perfect."

I wish she'd get on with it.

"So here it is." My mother sounds nervous now. This must be one expensive item. She reaches into the bag, rustles around in the tissue, and pulls out the most gorgeous little black dress I've ever seen. It's just like the Givenchy number that Audrey wore in *Breakfast at*

Tiffany's—slim and shiny, sleeveless, fitted in the waist and flaring into an adorable A-line.

"It's for you, Grace," she tells me, smiling. "For the awards dinner. It's like the one in your Audrey Hepburn poster. I thought you'd look just beautiful in it. Do you like it?"

I start to nod, but I feel too choked up to speak, and almost immediately—to my mother's distress—I burst into tears.

Chapter Ten

It's seven o'clock on the night of the Blue Lobster awards dinner, and I'm standing as still as I can while Sonia puffs perfumed blasts of hair spray around my head. The doorbell rings, and my father calls my name, telling me Hunter's arrived, but I want to check myself one last time in the mirror before I head down the stairs.

I can barely recognize the girl in front of me—she's so slim and elegant in the chic black dress, her hair swept up at the back with just a few tendrils escaping around her face, vintage diamante earrings sparkling, her eyes bright with happiness and anticipation. It's hard to believe that this is me: Grace di Giovanni of Cumberland, Connecticut, and not Holly Golightly or Sabrina. I slip into the black kitten heels my mother and I found at the mall after Thanksgiving, and Sonia dabs at my hair again, making sure it's just perfect.

"You look great, G," Sonia tells me, stepping back so

she's not blocking my view. "Shame it's going to be wasted on dinner with a bunch of football players at the Blue Lobster Grill."

"Shame it's only going to be for a few hours," I lament. By the time I unpin my hair and take off my makeup tonight, I'll have spent longer dressing and undressing than I spent at the actual event.

Downstairs, Hunter is chatting with my parents. When I begin my careful descent—I'm not used to heels, even tiny ones—they stop talking and look up at me. My parents are smiling, and however irritable Hunter's been about my going home early tonight, he looks pretty pleased right now, too.

"You're a knockout, Grace," says my father, and my mother squeals as though she smells something burning. There's no crisis—just the absence of a camera.

"You both look so cute," she says, after they tear the house apart looking for it. She makes us pose in front of the fireplace before we can leave. Hunter stands with a proprietary hand around my waist.

"You're beautiful," he whispers in my ear while my parents are preoccupied with getting the flash to work and Sonia is obligingly dragging Rascal out of the shot. Hunter looks really handsome in his suit—tall and smiling and confident. Really, I'm the luckiest girl in the school. Actually, right now I feel like the luckiest girl in the world.

"We should get going," I say to my parents after Hunter checks his watch for the third time. He's quite nervous about tonight, I can tell. I'm putting on my coat when Tom comes down the stairs and lopes into the kitchen. He's been in his room the whole time I was getting ready.

"Tom, come and take a look at your little sister," says my mother, beaming with pride. "She's just about to leave."

"Yeah, I saw her earlier," he says, without even bothering to turn around. This is a total lie: he never once stuck his head into my room. Tom doesn't say hi to Hunter or anything; he just swings open the fridge door and sticks his head inside.

"We need to go," Hunter murmurs.

My mother hugs me good-bye—carefully, so she doesn't mess my hair or crease my dress—and we step outside into the cold, crystal-clear night.

Everything seems like it's back to normal with me and Hunter, but that's mainly because we've avoided any more conversations about my leaving early tonight. I'm hoping that means he's okay with it. We haven't talked much about my audition in the morning either, though I sang "Since I Don't Have You" for him last week, and he said it sounded fantastic.

In the car we don't talk much, because he's so nervous about tonight. When we get to the restaurant—

taken over for the evening by Cumberland High and decorated with blue balloons and fake lobsters—he loosens up a whole lot, and is immediately swallowed up by a crowd of his teammates. They're all shouting, slapping each other's backs, and generally having a good time. Now it's my turn to feel nervous, because I really don't know any of these people. Our dates so far have been just the two of us—going to the movies or for a drive, or for a walk along the seafront or at the park. And none of these people, guys or girls, are really in my social circle. I wish Emily were here to hang out with me in a quiet corner and provide commentary. I try to fade into the background, but it's harder than usual because I'm all dressed up, and some girls are openly staring, probably trying to work out who I am. Two of them, both with long hair blow-dried super-straight, wearing strapless dresses and towering stilettos, walk over to me.

"Aren't you Sonia's sister?" one asks me, and I nod, giving a tentative smile. This is the fate of every younger sibling, I guess. I will be Sonia and Tom's little sister forever and ever.

"And you're here with . . . ?" the other one asks, looking me up and down.

"Hunter," I tell them. "Hunter Wells."

They exchange knowing looks.

"I'd heard he was seeing some girl," the first one says

to the other, as though I'm not even there. "I didn't realize it was . . . What's your name?"

"Grace," I say.

"And you're a junior, right?" asks the second girl. It feels as though their eyes are all over me, and that they don't entirely approve of what they see.

"Yup."

"I'm so annoyed with him for keeping you such a secret," says the first girl, though she doesn't look too annoyed. "I don't even remember seeing you at the games."

"Oh, I'm there," I say, but I'm not surprised they don't remember seeing me. First of all, I look completely different in my usual jeans-and-sweater ensemble, with my hair in a ponytail and no makeup on. And second, I always sit with Emily at games, and we don't hang around the locker room afterward, waiting for the boys to come out. It feels way too groupie-ish, and unnecessary—I'm usually seeing Hunter that evening, anyway. But now I'm wondering if this is something a good girlfriend—a real girlfriend—would do. Maybe it bothers Hunter that I'm not there at the end of every game to gush about how great he was.

"Your dress is real cute," says the second girl, and they both flash false smiles at me. And then they're gone, working their way through the milling groups, probably passing on the information to their friends. So much for my first conversation!

I try to spot Hunter, and see him at the other side of the big room, where the tables have been set up for dinner, deep in conversation with Coach Furtado and some other adults I don't recognize. Maybe one of them is the mayor of Cumberland; Hunter told me he was going to be here tonight. A photographer from the local paper is here, too, taking pictures of smiling, dressed-up Lobster players and their glam girlfriends. The sight of the tables with their white cloths and candles and rows of shiny cutlery makes me feel even more nervous. I hope I don't use the wrong fork or something, and embarrass myself. Even though we were dressing up, I didn't realize what a big deal this was going to be—all these dignitaries from the town, and this formal sit-down dinner. No wonder Hunter was all wound up; he's been to this event before.

And now I'm freaking out about something those girls said: that Hunter's been keeping me a big secret. I hope that doesn't mean he's ashamed of me in any way, or that he wanted to keep his options open. Maybe that's why he's never suggested hanging out together at lunchtime, why he's never taken me to any parties.

I feel like such a loser standing here by myself. I'd much rather be at home, hanging out with my family and thinking about the audition tomorrow. I'm trying to keep a smile on my face, but it's hard not to feel miserable.

"Sorry," says Hunter, materializing in front of me all of a sudden. "Coach wanted me to talk to some people from the Chamber of Commerce. Have you been standing here this whole time?"

"Sort of," I say, not wanting to sound completely lame. Hunter takes my hand.

"Come on, I want you to meet my buddies," he says, pulling me away from the wall. And now I feel both relieved and foolish. Of course Hunter isn't ashamed of me. He wouldn't have asked me here tonight if he were. I have to ignore the catty comments and just focus on having a good time.

After a slow, excruciating start to the evening, things improve. Hunter introduces me to a million people, and most of them seem friendly enough, even if their conversation is all about football and other people I don't know. Once we're seated for dinner, I feel less exposed, especially when it's clear that we're not going to be eating snails or lobster or some other difficult and/or messy food. It's just soup, then salad, and a main course of broiled fish—nothing even a klutz like me can't handle. After we're served dessert and coffee, Principal Thomas gets up to make a speech about the Blue Lobsters' great season and introduces Mayor

Myers, who talks for a long time about vague subjects like the vitality of youth and the rejuvenation of our community. Then Coach Furtado stands up to give a game-by-game rundown of the season, interrupted every few minutes by cheers and applause. I sneak a peek at my watch under the table—it's already nine, and none of the awards have been given out yet.

"How many awards are there?" I whisper to Hunter in a short break between speeches.

"About a dozen," he murmurs, squeezing my hand under the table. "The MVP will be announced last."

Hunter is so agitated, he doesn't even finish his dessert—that's not like him at all. Coach starts announcing the different awards and their winners, and the whole thing takes an agonizingly long time. Each award seems to have its own local sponsor, a representative who has to stand up and be acknowledged and make a presentation to the winner. There's even a special award for Ms. Schaeffer and her team of crazed decorators, sponsored by the local craft store. Finally, it's time for the MVP award. Coach Furtado shuffles the papers in his hands and asks the mayor to stand up again.

"Our last award of the evening goes to the player who's made the biggest difference this season, a player we're all real proud to call one of our own," says the coach. "He's played his last game as a Blue Lobster, but

I have a pretty good hunch he'll be playing a whole lot of football next year. Many of the scouts who've come through Cumberland have been real impressed with what they've seen, and unless I'm losing my mind, which is always a possibility, in just a few weeks this player is going to be getting some big offers."

Everyone in the room whoops and hollers. Hunter's hand, back to gripping mine under the table, feels clammy.

"So this year it's Cumberland High," continues the coach. "And next year, who knows? If I were a betting man, I'd have my money on the University of Michigan or Notre Dame."

People start drumming on their tables, and I glance at Hunter. His face is flushed pink, turned toward the speaker.

"So with no further ado," says Coach Furtado, holding up one hand for quiet, "I'll ask the mayor to present this year's MVP award to a big star with a big future—Hunter Wells!"

Everyone in the room goes wild. Hunter stands up slowly, the napkin on his lap falling to the ground, and makes his way, head down, across the room. I'm so happy for him: I clap so hard my hands start to sting. This is what he wanted so badly, and if what Coach says comes true, he's going to get the football scholarship he's been dreaming about. If anyone deserves a dream come true, it's Hunter—he's worked really hard for it. Up there, shaking hands with the mayor, holding up his plaque for everyone to see, he looks bashful and overwhelmed. I wish Tom could see him now; maybe then he'd quit thinking Hunter is some arrogant jock. He's really a sensitive person who gives his all to things he believes in. By comparison, my brother's a total slacker. Maybe it's the comparison that bothers him.

It takes a while for Hunter to wend his way back to me, because everyone wants to congratulate him; and also kids are standing up now, getting ready to head off to the after-party.

"Where we can really celebrate," says the guy sitting across from me, winking and tapping his pocket. He's got a hip flask in there; I can see the brass cap sticking out. "Everyone knows it's at Joey's, right?"

I nod and smile, playing along about going, but my heart is sinking. It's well after ten, and by the time I get out of here, arrive home, and take all my makeup off, it'll be eleven. We all got "Get Out of School Free" cards earlier in the evening, which means the Blue Lobsters and their guests aren't expected at school tomorrow until noon, but I still have to be there just after nine. Mrs. Lane wants all auditioning girls to arrive at least fifteen minutes before their time slot. And I'd like to do some warm-up exercises in the bathroom before it's my turn, to make sure my voice isn't all croaky and cold.

I've tried to explain this to Hunter—that it's just like him warming up his muscles before a game, as well as getting in the right mental space so you're ready to perform.

Part of me desperately wants to stay with Hunter right now, to stand by his side at the party, bask in his glow, and tell him how proud I am of him. When he reaches me at last, I give him a big hug.

"You deserve it," I say, and he gives me a huge smile, relaxed and relieved.

"Let's go," he says, and we start the slow shuffle to the front door of the restaurant. I make it first, of course, because lots of people still want to shake Hunter's hand and slap him on the back. I retrieve my coat and wait patiently by the front door, holding Hunter's coat over my arm. The two girls who talked to me earlier pass by on their way out.

"See you at Joey's!" they call to me, as though I'm suddenly their best friend. A chilly blast of air hits me when the door pushes open, and my heart sinks. Maybe I should go to the party for just a little while. But then I'll have to drag Hunter away when he's enjoying himself to give me a ride home, and the earliest I'll get to bed is midnight. I'll just be sabotaging my own chances in the audition tomorrow, throwing everything away just for a party. Sure, it's not just *any* party, I argue to myself. This is a special night for Hunter. But he doesn't need me there to make it special. I know he'll be okay with dropping me off at home before he goes to Joey's.

He's not okay.

"You won't even come for an hour?" he demands when we're in the car and he's adjusting the heat. It's turned into a really cold night.

"You know I would at any other time," I say. "Really, I'm so bummed about this, I can't tell you."

"I can't believe you're springing this on me now, Grace," he grumbles, pulling out of his parking space and roaring up to a red light.

"I'm not! We talked about it weeks ago!"

"But you never said another word about it. I thought you'd changed your mind."

"Hunter, my audition is at *nine thirty* tomorrow. . . ."

"And you'll do great. I heard you sing—you're fantastic."

"Not first thing in the morning, and not after I haven't had enough sleep, and not after a party where people are smoking and I have to shout to make myself heard!"

"Okay, okay," he says. The smile of ten minutes earlier is completely gone. "I'm taking you home, just like you want."

He swerves off the main road and drives too fast up the hill.

"You know I'd give anything to spend the rest of the evening with you," I say unhappily. "But this audition is really important to me."

"Yeah, I know," he replies. "I understand it's your *priority* right now."

"Please don't be sarcastic," I plead. "It's only an issue today and tomorrow—then it'll all be over."

"Until you get the leading role, and then you'll have rehearsals all the time, and the show will be your priority, not me."

"Of course I'll have time for you!" This is such an awful conversation. I can't believe this is how the evening is ending. Hunter says nothing, and I don't dare open my mouth again. I'm upset with myself for spoiling his evening, and I'm upset with him for being so extreme and irrational. When he pulls up outside my house, I don't get out.

"I don't want to go in while you're still angry with me," I say, turning to face him.

"I'm not angry." He looks down at his hands on the wheel. "I'm just disappointed."

A pang of guilt knots my stomach.

"I'm really sorry," I whisper, and lean toward him for a kiss.

Hunter stays rigid, not looking at me. I plant a kiss on his cheek and wait to see if he relents. But he doesn't move. It's like he can't wait for me to get out of the car—maybe out of his life, too. I open the door and climb out, pulling my coat tight around me. He doesn't walk me to the door, like he usually does; he doesn't even wait for me to reach the porch before zooming off down the hill. I stand at the door shivering, fumbling for my house key. This isn't the way this evening was supposed to turn out.

Chapter Eleven

It's nine o'clock on Monday morning, and I'm sitting on the floor outside the school auditorium. Next to me is Emily, who has the audition slot before mine. She's wearing her lucky rust-colored sweater, and her wayward curls are bunched up in a bouncy ponytail. I haven't said much to her about last night, because thinking about my fight with Hunter makes me feel sick to my stomach. Maybe it's just audition nerves combined with guilt about refusing to go to the after-party, but deep down I'm glad I didn't go; I feel tired this morning as it is, worn out with the excitement and upheaval of yesterday, not to mention feeling anxious about today, and my eyes are still red and scoured from crying after I climbed into bed last night.

All around us are other girls, some from the drama club, some I barely recognize. Most are sitting around chatting in low voices. One or two are doing warm-up stretches, even though it's a singing audition and we've been told we won't have to dance. Another sits against the wall, earphones in, her iPod clutched in one hand. She's trying to zone everyone else out, I suppose, and focus on the song she's about to sing. I'm not surprised she wants to zone out; there's a real tension in the air today. It's usually not like this at auditions. Sure, there's an atmosphere of nervousness and anticipation, but today you'd think we were auditioning for a Broadway show itself, rather than just a Broadway director.

"Maybe I should sing something different." Emily is fretting about her choice of song—"Secret Love," a fifties ballad by another of our absolute, all-time favorites, Doris Day. She's been freaking out about this all week, obsessing over whether she should sing a song from *Grease* itself or something more contemporary. This fit came over her when she heard that not one but two girls in our class were planning to sing the Britney Spears song "Toxic," complete with self-choreographed dance steps.

"Your song is great," I reassure her. "It's too late to change now anyway. You need to sing something you're confident about."

"I should have picked something faster," she laments. "You know I get all wobbly in slow songs."

"You'll be fine," I say, squeezing her arm. And just at

that moment a girl comes out of the auditorium and tells Emily to go in. "Break a leg!"

"Knowing my luck, I will," she mutters, and scrambles to her feet, dusting invisible dust off her jeans. She takes a deep breath, pushes open the door, and disappears into the giant auditorium. Jessica, the girl who's just auditioned, hangs around to tell us about her experience.

"Nick Smart just sat there tapping his head with a pencil, literally the whole time I was singing," she says, looking dejected. "Mrs. Lane didn't even smile once."

Great. Even Mrs. Lane is feeling the pressure. Maybe Nick Smart is in despair about the lack of talent at Cumberland High and is about to walk off the job in protest.

"Did he ask you any questions?" another girl asks her.

Jessica shakes her head. "He just kind of mumbled 'thanks' when I finished. And then he said something else, and I thought he was talking to me, but Mrs. Lane said they were just talking about sending someone out to Starbucks for some more coffee."

"I'll go!" calls Chiara, a member of the Nick Smart Fan Club. She can't sing or dance, but she's determined to audition just so she can have his undivided attention for five minutes. These girls are crazy. He's not even that cute!

"Ms. Schaeffer already went," Jessica tells her.

I'm not sure why Ms. Schaeffer is hanging around the auditions, unless she's in the Nick Smart Fan Club, too.

I close my eyes and try to get my brain together. My heart is racing, and although I'm trying really hard, it's impossible to get Hunter's face out of my head. Last night, when he said I'd disappointed him, I felt completely crushed. I've never had to choose between anything before, unless you count pairs of jeans or flavors of ice cream; everything in my life has been pretty straightforward. Now things seem like a complicated balancing act. If this is what it's like to be an adult, then it sucks.

Pull yourself together, Grace, I tell myself. Miss Sara would go crazy if she knew you were squandering these last precious moments before an audition worrying about a boy. To be an artist, you need to have focus. That's what she said over and over again. And you need to have daring—the courage to try things and the courage to risk failure. This is the really hard part for me. My knees are knocking at the very thought of standing up and walking down through the auditorium and onto the stage. And that's just for an audience of three—Mrs. Lane, Nick Smart, and Mr. Fisher, who's our rehearsal pianist and is almost a hundred years old. What will I be like if I'm ever in the spotlight doing a solo number in front of hundreds of people?

It was stage fright that spoiled my chances last year—I know it. I got up on the stage and started to sing my audition piece, and my voice began to crack and waver. My head felt like it was burning off my shoulders and about to explode into the ceiling. And I was so preoccupied with just getting through the song, I forgot to move at all. I just stood glued to the spot, my hands by my side. It was so awful, I was lucky to even get a role in the chorus. During the course of rehearsals and shows, I totally loosened up and became more confident, and Mrs. Lane told me I'd become a really good performer. And of course, this summer at camp I improved like two hundred percent, but I'm still nervous about taking a step back today, of not having the courage that Miss Sara talked about.

The door swings open, and a flushed Emily emerges.

"You're up, G," she says, and I grab all my stuff, pulling my sheet music from the front pocket of my backpack.

"How did it go?" I ask her, pausing outside the door.

"Okay," she says, sounding uncertain, and then she shoots me a plucky smile. "You'll do great. Knock 'em dead."

"I'll try," I whisper, and step into the cool dimness of the auditorium. I walk down the aisle, past rows of empty seats, trying to take each step slowly so I don't fall or disgrace myself in some way before I even get onstage. *Keep your head high*, Miss Sara would say—she was big on audition advice. *Let them know you're proud of your talents and abilities before you even open your mouth to sing. There's nothing arrogant about poise, and there's nothing admirable about slouching.* Easy for Miss Sara to say. She's not tall and gangly with a tendency to trip over her own feet.

Mrs. Lane and Nick Smart are sitting about a dozen rows back, deep in conversation, as I climb the stairs to the stage and hand Mr. Fisher my music.

"Hello, Grace!" calls Mrs. Lane, apparently noticing me for the first time. "Nick, this is Grace di Giovanni."

She lowers her voice and starts muttering to him. She's probably telling him how I fall apart under pressure and lack the maturity for a starring role.

"So, Grace," says Nick Smart, scratching his head with the pencil Jessica mentioned. I blink at him. He's all in black today, and the light is reflecting off his glasses, so he looks kind of creepy. "You're our thirteenth audition this morning. Number thirteen, lucky for some—right?"

"Yeah, right," I reply, and cough a little, quickly raising my hand to my mouth. Even though I've been sipping water while I waited, my mouth feels dry, and I'm almost light-headed with nerves. I clench and release my fingers, trying to get rid of some of the tension in my body.

"What are you singing for us today?" Mrs. Lane shuffles the papers on her lap. She seems distracted, bored already with the endless ranks of hopeful girls parading on and off the stage. What was it Miss Sara said? *Don't think about the people in the room; just focus on yourself, in the spotlight, singing to that invisible audience member in the back row of the balcony. Project, project, project.*

"I'm going to sing 'Since I Don't Have You,'" I tell them, and the way my voice sounds—clear and confident all of a sudden, ringing through the expanse of the auditorium—surprises me. This is something Miss Sara made us practice at camp—announcing a number in a loud voice, chin raised high in the air—and it felt totally ridiculous then. But here, standing on a stage, facing the long rows of seats, I see why she got us to do it. Both Mrs. Lane and Nick Smart seem to sit up a little, and they look like they're really paying attention.

"Whenever you're ready," Nick says, leaning forward with his arms dangling over the seat in front of him, the pencil of boredom nowhere in sight. I glance at Mr. Fisher and nod; he plays the first bars of the song, and I take a deep, deep breath.

"I don't have plans and schemes," I sing, staying true

on the long first note. *"And I don't have hopes and dreams."*

My voice rings out, sweet and high-pitched, not wavering at all. And then it happens: the song pours out and I lose myself in it, just the way I do when I'm singing at home in my bedroom. I forget about the two people scrutinizing me. I forget that my feet feel like lead, and instead I take a few steps this way and that, one hand rising and falling in a flowing gesture. And I keep my focus on the words of the song: *"I don't have anything, since I don't have you,"* making the most of this moment, not worrying about how I sound or look or come across. Just being myself.

Think of me in the back row if that helps, Miss Sara said. *Imagine me sitting there, smiling at you, loving every single second of your performance.* So I do, and it does. I lift my head and sing to the invisible Miss Sara, imagining her big goofy smile, her eyes sparkling with pleasure. But I can hear her cajoling me: *Make me feel it, now—make me feel the song.* I sing, and all the sadness and confusion I felt last night after I said good-bye to Hunter is there, right there in the song. *"When you walked out on me, in walked old misery."* Maybe that's how he saw it—me walking out on him. For the first time, I'm singing like I really mean it, maybe because now I'm experiencing these emotions, not just thinking about them.

Then, just like that, the song is over. Mr. Fisher plays

the last quiet notes, and the room is silent. All my jitters return in a huge rush when I look down at Mrs. Lane and Nick Smart. I can't tell anything from the expressions on their faces; maybe they thought I was too over the top.

"Thank you, Grace," says Mrs. Lane. "Would you ask Chiara to give us a few minutes before she comes in?"

"Sure, Mrs. Lane. Thanks," I say, but she and Nick have already bent their heads together and are talking in low voices. I collect my music from Mr. Fisher, heave my bag onto my shoulder, and trudge back up the stairs to the main door. It's all over, thank goodness, and whether they liked me or not, at least I did my best. I didn't freak out, I didn't crumble, and I didn't get all tongue-tied and crazy.

"Well?" demands Emily when I'm back in the crowded lobby and I've told Chiara to hang on for a while. She's pleased to have the extra time, because her friend is still spraying silver dye onto her hair. She wants to make a big impression on Nick Smart.

"Okay, I think," I tell Emily, shrugging. "Pretty well. They didn't say anything."

"That doesn't mean anything," she says. "They can't start giving out high scores until the Olympic champions appear on the ice later on."

Emily is really into ice-skating—i.e. watching it on TV—and often makes skating analogies. By Olympic champions, I presume she means the senior girls, like Terri Cooper.

"You see, they can't say stuff like 'You've totally got the part' until the old guard arrives and they all fall on their butts trying to do a triple toe loop," she explains as we head off to class, away from the nervous gaggle still waiting for their turn onstage. "Old Nick Smart has to play his cards close to his vest."

After the audition, I'm so tired and deflated, I feel like I'm dozing through school all day. Classes are disrupted anyway, with people disappearing off to audition, and late arrivals rolling in, clutching their "Get Out of School Free" cards. That evening I call Hunter to tell him about how it went, but his voice mail picks up every time I try his number. Either he's turned his phone off or he just doesn't want to speak to me, and I'm almost too exhausted at this point to care. My mother suggests that I have an early night, and I'm very happy to comply.

On Tuesday morning, the school is buzzing with predictions about how people did in the auditions, who's getting which part, and a rumor—probably completely untrue—that Nick Smart stormed out in a rage during the boys' auditions, screaming that he couldn't stand to hear another oaf butchering a Stevie Wonder song.

"Dude, he's evil, like Simon Cowell," one of the boys in my homeroom tells me. "I've heard he's not going to let anyone from the school appear in the show. He's going to bring in all the performers from Broadway."

I roll my eyes.

"I heard that he asked every girl for her number," says another of my idiot classmates. "And if she refused, then she's not getting a part in the show."

At lunchtime, Emily and I are walking to the cafeteria when Jessica and some of her friends sprint past us, running toward the drama club room.

"G, results must be posted," says Emily, grabbing my arm and swinging me around. And then we run, too, pushing through the crowds of kids headed to lunch, catching up with Jessica and her crew. Sure enough, on the notice board outside, there's a white sheet posted with GREASE CASTING LIST in huge letters. It's already surrounded by people, everyone pointing and smudging the type with their greasy fingers, some of them squealing with delight, some shouting expletives when they don't see their name on the list. Emily shoves me forward so my nose almost hits the board, and the first name I see on the list is the boy playing the lead role of Danny. No surprise: it's Greg Maxwell, who's had the lead every year for the past three. My heart sinks. That probably means he'll be paired with Terri Cooper

128

again. Her name should be next on the list, right below his.

But instead I see my name. I blink, and yup—it's still there. Sandy . . . Grace di Giovanni. I'm playing the lead. I'm going to be Sandy!

Chapter Twelve

So I'm not even going to try and hide it: I'm unbelievably psyched. As much as I'd hoped things would turn out this way, I didn't really believe it was possible. When I read my name up there on the cast list, I think maybe I'm seeing things. But then I hear Emily shrieking "Oh my God! You got it!" and the girls around me, their faces a blur, saying "Congratulations, Grace" and "Good job."

Another surge in the crowd pushes me away before I get a chance to see any of the other names on the list. I'm still in a daze when Emily emerges from the cluster and pulls me away down the hall. That's when I start coming back down to earth, really. Emily's name is up there, too, she tells me, but just in the general chorus list. She's trying to be cheerful and pretend it doesn't matter, and that the main thing is we're both in the show, but I know she's kind of bummed.

"You did it, G," she keeps telling me as we walk to the

cafeteria. "You aced the audition, just like we planned. This is going to be our year after all. I'm throwing the backup plan away."

"What was the backup plan again?" I ask, linking my arm through hers.

"It was blank," she confesses. "I had total faith in you all along. Oh my God!"

"What?" We both stop dead.

"You get to kiss Greg Maxwell! That means by the end of this school year you'll have achieved the rare double play."

"I don't even want to ask what you're talking about." I tug Emily's arm to get her moving again. Suddenly I'm ravenously hungry.

"I mean, you'll have kissed not one but two A-listers: Hunter Wells and Greg Maxwell. It's a total coup. It's the highest possible achievement any girl could hope for in her junior year."

"You know, I did pretty well on the PSAT too," I say drily.

"Like that matters," she says, rolling her eyes, and we both start giggling, hurrying to get in line at the cafeteria before all the pizza is gone.

It's nice to make my parents happy, I have to say; though they were more appreciative of my good PSAT score than Emily was.

"Here's to Grace," my father says at dinner that night, and everyone holds up their water glasses, clinking them in a typically noisy way so drops of water splatter over the food. "Honey, we are so proud of you. You're going to be the star of the show, and it's a triumph very well deserved."

"Here, here," says my mother, who's had a huge smile on her face ever since I arrived from school and told her the news.

"Hey, Gracie," says Tom, who's acting like his normal self for a change. "I hear that Greg Maxwell has really bad breath, and that he likes to slip his leading ladies the tongue."

"That's delightful," complains my father, his mouth full of baked potato, gesturing at my mother with his fork. "See the kind of things your son says?"

"Just ignore him." I help myself to more green beans. "He thinks all guys have to resort to his own desperate tactics to get a girl to kiss them."

"Yeah, what was the name of your last girlfriend, Tom?" teases Sonia. "It was so long ago, none of us can remember."

"I'm just warning little Gracie here," he says. "Unless she wants to get some of Maxwell's Summer Lovin' . . ."

"Shut up!"

"That's not nice, Tom," says my mother. "Let's just have a nice dinner for once."

"Oh God," drones Sonia. "I suppose this means Grace is going to be playing the *Grease* sound track all day every day over Christmas vacation and singing along at the top of her voice."

"Maybe you can do one of your big numbers for the family at Christmas?" my father suggests, and I immediately start protesting. There are going to be at least forty members of the extended di Giovanni family at my grandmother's house this year, and I don't want to make an exhibit of myself.

"Make them buy tickets," says Tom, reaching over my plate for the salt and pretending to elbow me in the face at the same time. I push his arm away. "Why should they get to hear Grace for free? Cumberland High needs their money."

"That's the first sensible thing you've said tonight," I tell him.

After dinner, when I'm back in the calm of my bedroom, I try calling Hunter again. There's still no reply.

"Hey, it's me," I say to his voice mail. "I really want to talk to you. The cast list went up today, and I wanted to tell you . . . well, I'd rather tell *you*, not your machine. So call me back, okay? I miss you, and I still feel really bad about Sunday night. Bye."

All evening I wait for him to call. I even go downstairs at one point and call my own cell phone from the phone in the hall, just to make sure it's working. Rascal seems to sense I need company, so he pads up the stairs and into my room. He flops with a heavy sigh onto the floor next to my bed. Sonia, who's walking past at that moment, pauses in my doorway.

"Hey," she says, pulling off her reading glasses and rubbing her eyes. "What does Hunter think about you getting the part?"

"He . . . well, he doesn't know about it yet," I tell her. "At least, he hasn't heard it from me. Someone else might have told him."

"What's up with you two?" Sonia asks, frowning.

"Nothing," I say, and that miserable feeling from Sunday night descends on me again. "He's just . . . he's mad at me, I think. About coming home early after the awards dinner and not going to the party with him."

"He knew about your audition, *mais oui*?"

"Yeah, I guess. Yeah, he did."

"Then what was his problem? Didn't he want you to get the part?"

"Oh, he did," I say quickly, leaping to Hunter's defense. "I know he did. I know he's going to be really proud of me."

This is a lie. I don't know if he's going to be proud of me or not. I don't know what's going on in Hunter's head right now. Maybe he never wants to see me again. This thought makes me feel even more miserable.

"So what's his deal?" Sonia looks puzzled.

"He was just disappointed, that's all," I say, knowing how lame it sounds. "It was a big night for him."

"Listen, Gracie," says Sonia, giving one of her brisk sniffs. "Hunter needs to get over himself. Sure it was a big night for him, but it was a big night for you, too—the night before your audition. You made the mature decision to get home at a reasonable time so you wouldn't feel like hell the next day. And it paid off. You did the right thing. He wouldn't stay out late if he was playing football at nine the next morning, with someone important coming to judge his performance, would he?"

I shake my head and stare down at the carpet. Rascal thinks I'm looking at him, so he thumps his tail, hoping I'll pay attention to him. I know Sonia's trying to be nice, but I wish she'd leave. I feel like crying.

"Don't be upset," Sonia says. "He's just a guy. You're going to meet plenty more like him—better than him—when you go to college. The thing is, Hunter's a jock. To him, football is everything. He'll never understand you have different priorities. He just wants you there on the sidelines cheering him on. Don't let him bring you down, okay? He's not worth it. This should be a happy day for you."

She takes a few steps into my room to ruffle my hair in a show of sisterly camaraderie, and then retreats off down the hallway. I want to tell her that she has Hunter all wrong, that he's more than just a selfish jock. But part of me wonders if she's right—if Hunter would really prefer me to be like those other Blue Lobster girls, hanging around outside the locker room after a game, thinking of nothing but their boyfriends and the team.

But how can Sonia say that Hunter's not worth it? She has no idea how great it is when we spend time together, how easy it is for us to talk, how relaxed and content and happy I am. I've never felt this way about a boy before. Sure, I've had crushes—on Justin Timberlake; on Mr. Matteo, my ninth-grade biology teacher; and even, briefly, on this cute boy named Robbie at theater camp this summer. Hunter is different. It's not about me obsessing over a picture in a magazine or someone who's completely unattainable. He's a real live guy who takes me to the movies and hangs out on the porch with me, a guy who opens the car door so I can get in, who holds my hand when we go for walks. We can talk about anything and everything, and when I'm with him I feel beautiful. I know that sounds silly and conceited, but what I mean is this: when he looks at me, his eyes shining, I feel like he sees something in me that nobody in the world does, not even my parents. He sees a Grace who's not a little girl, not the youngest kid or a little sister. He sees *me*, the way I am now, the way I want to be. This is too good a feeling to let go. I leave him another message before I go to bed, and decide that tomorrow at school, no matter what, I'm going to track Hunter down.

Either Hunter's not at school today or he's gone into serious hiding, but I don't see him anywhere, and everyone I ask shrugs and says they don't know where he is. I hope everything's okay. I'm starting to feel frantic because he's not returning my calls, and even when I hang around his locker like a Blue Lobster groupie, I don't see him.

When I get home from school, my mood swings from elated, every time I think about the show, to depressed, when I remember that Hunter is avoiding me. I mope around for a while in the kitchen, watching my mother prepare dinner—baked ziti with spinach and ricotta, one of my favorites—and then, after she tells me she doesn't need any help, I sit at the breakfast bar pretending to read my history textbook. It's impossible to concentrate, mainly because I keep glancing over at my cell phone, willing it to ring.

It doesn't ring, of course, but something else does, not long after five: the doorbell. My mother asks me to get it, because she's busy rinsing something off in the sink.

"Your brother keeps forgetting his key," she sighs, so

I wriggle down from the stool and slide across the floor in my socks, still waiting for the call.

When I pull the door open, flinching at the blast of cold air, all I can see is a big bunch of rust-colored chrysanthemums wrapped in cellophane. And then the flowers move down and Hunter emerges from behind them, the rueful grin on his face making him look totally adorable.

"Delivery for Miss Grace di Giovanni," he says, thrusting the bouquet toward me, and I start laughing with relief and happiness. Hunter's not angry at me anymore—everything's okay. "I hear she's going to be big on Broadway one of these days."

"Very funny," I say, pulling him over the threshold and into the warm house. I'm thrilled with the bouquet: nobody's ever bought me flowers before. "Let me show my mother."

"Grace, wait." He holds on to my arm. "I want to tell you something. It's a secret. The only people who know so far are my mom and Coach. I got a call today from the University of Michigan. They're going to make me an offer!"

"That's fantastic," I say, trying to keep my voice down. "But didn't you want to be somewhere closer to home?"

"Yeah," he says, but he doesn't sound very certain. "That would have been ideal. But Michigan is a great school and a great team. And they're going to give me the kind of scholarship I've dreamed about—it's a full ride."

"I'm so happy for you," I whisper, and he hugs me, almost crushing the flowers. "I wish you didn't have to go so far away."

I guess Hunter doesn't hear this, because he just keeps talking about how excited he is, reminding me I have to keep the news to myself until he gets a written offer. He doesn't say anything about Sunday night, or why he hasn't returned any of my calls, and I certainly don't want to bring it up now. All is forgiven, that's pretty clear.

"It's a big week for me, Grace," he says, ruffling my hair.

"For both of us," I tell him, smiling, and for just a moment he looks kind of confused. "I got the part, remember?"

"Yeah, yeah," he says, hugging me close again.

I'm so happy that he's here, that things have worked out for him, that he's not mad at me anymore. But in the back of my mind there's a niggling question: would he have come over to congratulate me, acting like we never had a fight at all, if he hadn't had such good news of his own?

Chapter Thirteen

The holidays fly by, my entire break consumed by Christmas shopping, helping my parents cook huge quantities of food, and spending too many days with too many cousins and aunts and uncles. Between family activities and a heap of homework, I barely have a minute to myself. Whenever I can grab a moment, I practice one of my numbers for the show. I even make myself stand in front of the mirror when I sing—highly embarrassing, but necessary, according to Miss Sara, if you want to make sure you're not frowning or squinting or looking dorky.

I don't get to see much of Hunter, because he's away visiting his grandparents in Wisconsin for most of the holidays. When he gets back, we exchange gifts. I've never bought something for a boyfriend before, so I decide to play it safe and get him a scarf. He looks pretty disappointed with this, I have to say. He gave me some perfume—it probably cost him a ton, but it smells gross, all sweet and floral. I have to pretend to like it, though, because I don't want to hurt his feelings.

And now it's a brand new year, complete with just enough snow to make the streets look pretty, but not enough to keep us home from school, and way too much homework to make going out much of an option. On one sharp, sunny Saturday, Tom lures me away from the books and out into the yard to build an ominous-looking snowman, complete with a Blue Lobster scarf and hat. But Rascal keeps barking at it, thinking it's an intruder, and after a couple of days it collapses on one side; some local kids finish it off by kicking it into icy lumps.

The teachers piling on the homework don't care one iota that Mrs. Lane has set rehearsals for principals twice a week after school, plus Sunday afternoons. This doesn't include my weekly singing lesson, of course, which my voice coach has moved to Saturday mornings. My life is a bigger whirlwind than any of the snowstorms we've had so far, and things are about to get crazier. Mrs. Lane tell us that Nick Smart is going to start attending the weekend rehearsals in order to whip us into shape, and we need to have several key scenes and production numbers together before he descends from on high—or from down south, strictly speaking, as he lives in New York City.

It's hard to find time for a personal life with all these demands from school. I still see Emily every day in class, but as a chorus member, she just has to come to two rehearsals a week, and most of the time we're rehearsing in different rooms. She's incredibly busy, too, because of the photography work she's doing for the school newspaper. It may not be getting her into A-list parties like she'd planned, but it sure seems to entail attending a lot of editorial meetings and school events.

We don't even have lunch together much anymore. Now that football season is over, and Hunter has more free time, he wants to hang out with me at lunchtime. For a while the three of us ate together, but I think Emily was a little uncomfortable with the way Hunter would want to hold my hand all the time, or start nuzzling against my neck while Emily and I were in the middle of a conversation.

"Tell you what—I'll leave you two lovebirds alone," she said one day, and picked up her tray and left before I could say anything. From then on, most days she drifted away to be with her newspaper buddies, telling me they had stuff to discuss. Hunter didn't even pretend to be bothered by this. It's not that he doesn't like Emily—he thinks she's kind of weird, maybe, but he's never complained about her.

"I want you all to myself," he complains. "You see Emily all day long."

"But we can't talk in class," I try to tell him.

"Sure you can," he says. "And between classes, too. I'm with you for, like, thirty minutes a day."

Don't get me wrong: I love spending lunchtime with Hunter. I really enjoy his company, and sitting with him in the cafeteria is a whole different experience from eating lunch with Emily. So many people come by to say hi, or invite us to things. And because practically the whole school not only knows who Hunter is, but knows about him getting the big football scholarship to Michigan, lots of kids stare at us. It's a strange experience for me, suddenly being one of the A-listers, someone who other people look at and talk about and maybe even envy. Oh, I know that it's a stupid thing to care about, but I can't help enjoying the attention just a little, basking in the Hunter Wells glow. Maybe I'll have a glow of my own, eventually, after people see me up on the stage.

I do miss having the time to gossip and scheme and joke around with Emily. And after only a few weeks of rehearsals, I notice that it's not just the school newspaper crowd she's hanging out with—it's other girls from the chorus.

"We're having so much fun learning the songs and the dance steps," she tells me after I wait for her to finish some big conversation so we can walk to social studies together. "We're still pretty hopeless, or at least

I am. But Ms. Schaeffer says we're making great progress."

Ms. Schaeffer has wriggled her way into the show, of course. Mrs. Lane gave us a big speech about Ms. Schaeffer's strengths in large-scale choreography, and how she represented her college at the National Cheerleading Championships back in olden times. This means, apparently, that Ms. Schaeffer has license to boss around the chorus and teach them how to look overanimated while jumping around onstage. This leaves Mrs. Lane free to work with the principals in another room.

"It's not so much fun for us right now," I tell Emily. "We're doing lots of intensive acting workshops so we can learn our lines and get to know our characters."

"Is Terri totally out of control?" Emily asks.

Terri Cooper has been cast "against type," as Mrs. Lane keeps telling her, as Rizzo, the supercool nemesis of my character, Sandy.

"Let's just say she's taking the whole Rizzo/Sandy rivalry very seriously," I say as we stroll into the classroom and dump our books onto adjacent desks. "She's got the whole personal animosity thing down already. I'm afraid she's going to stab me one night onstage."

"Or knock you out with her ponytail. By the way, have you kissed Greg Maxwell yet?"

"No!"

"Well, let me know when it's scheduled, and I'll come in and take a picture for the paper."

"Haven't you got anything better to do?" I ask her, rolling my eyes.

"Not really," sighs Emily. "Ms. Schaeffer said it's a pity I'm not taller, because if I were she could stick me in the back row, where nobody could see me making mistakes."

Meanwhile, my parents are nagging me about not neglecting my schoolwork, running myself ragged, burning myself out, etc.

"There are only so many hours in the day, Grace," my father says one night after dinner when he and I are unloading the dishwasher.

"Maybe you need to make more time for yourself," urges my mother. I don't know how I'm supposed to make time out of thin air. "You're being pulled in so many different directions."

"But, Ma, I thought you were happy about my getting the part."

"We're delighted," my mother tells me. "And we understand that it's going to take up most of your free time for the next few months."

"So maybe you need to . . . you know, open up your schedule a little," says my father, wincing as he stands up because his back always aches in cold weather. "Reduce your other commitments."

Now I get it.

"You want me to stop seeing Hunter?" I'm totally incredulous.

"Maybe just cool it a little," suggests my mother. "Just for a while, until the show is over and your life returns to normal. You can see him at school, and maybe go out now and then. . . ."

"Now and then?" Do my parents have any idea about how a relationship works? Hunter would freak out if he could hear this.

"It's just that things always seem up and down with you two," my mother continues. Great. That's the last time I ever confide in Sonia—she totally tattled to my parents. "That can turn into a real emotional drain. Maybe this relationship isn't the best thing for you."

"Everything's fine," I say. "You don't understand. Hunter really cares about me."

My mother closes the cutlery drawer and exchanges concerned looks with my father.

"If he really does care about you, he'll understand that you need this time. We just feel like you're knocking yourself out to see him every week and, well, I don't know if he'd do the same for you, honey."

"You are so wrong about him," I say, slapping a dish towel down on the kitchen counter. "You don't know him at all. Look, I can't talk about this right now. I have a ton of homework to finish."

"Just think about it, okay?" my mother calls as I scamper up the stairs.

Yeah, right. Like I can put a boyfriend like Hunter—my first real boyfriend, for God's sake—on hold for three months. I close my bedroom door and walk to the window, gazing into the evening sky.

"I don't have love to share, and I don't have one who cares," I sing softly, my voice cracking on the words. My parents have no idea how unhappy I'd be without Hunter. Why do they have to make everything more difficult than it already is?

The last Sunday in February, Nick Smart turns up at our rehearsals for the first time. The whole cast assembles in the big rehearsal room to show him where we're at with the opening number, and then we break into our different rooms, as usual, and he wanders in and out. Half the time he's talking on his cell phone or conducting muttered conversations with Mrs. Lane and the other teachers helping to drill us into shape. But he does spend some time with me and Greg Maxwell, asking to hear our lines from the drive-in movie scene. He doesn't just sit in a chair watching us, the way Mrs. Lane does: Nick paces around us like a polar bear, rubbing his chin and frowning. I'm afraid he's going to blast us when it's over, but instead he's full of really helpful suggestions about the way we're standing or the way we're delivering our lines, and he asks us questions about our characters and actually waits to hear what we have to say.

"Phew," Greg says to me when Nick finally leaves the room. "That was way more nerve-racking than performing in front of hundreds of people."

Mrs. Lane is all smiles.

"You did great," she tells us. "Nick is very impressed."

When rehearsals finish, I walk outside and look around for my dad. The Blue Lobster Cadillac is nowhere to be seen, but Hunter's car is parked on the far side of the lot, and he flashes his headlights to get my attention.

"I told your father I'd pick you up," he says after I run over and climb in.

"That's nice," I say, pressing my cold nose against his cheek and giving him a kiss, hoping my parents didn't give him any grief about wanting to spend time with me.

Maybe they did, because there's clearly something wrong. Hunter drives out into the slushy street, staring at the road ahead with a grim, determined look on his face. I start nervously blabbing on about rehearsal and the things Nick Smart said.

"He talked a whole lot about commitment and focus and energy," I say. "You could tell he was surprised that we knew all our lines. Mrs. Lane was proud of us for being so 'on.' And when he got me and Greg to do part of one scene, he said he was really impressed with the way we were interacting. I didn't think it went so well, really—we've done a much better job in rehearsals, but . . . what?"

Hunter is shaking his head like he can't believe what he's hearing.

"What's wrong?" I ask him, dreading his answer. I hope my parents didn't pull some stunt and threaten to take out a restraining order against him or anything.

"So I guess it's true, then."

"What? What's true?"

"What everyone's saying about you and Maxwell."

"What?"

"That you're running after him like a love-struck little girl."

"Hunter!" This wasn't what I was expecting at all. "What are you talking about?"

"You know," he says, glaring at the steering wheel.

"No, I don't know, actually," I argue. This is the craziest thing I've ever heard. "Whoever's saying these things to you is just trying to cause trouble."

"I've heard it from more than one person," he snaps.

"So, let me guess—that means Terri Cooper and one of her friends, right?" He doesn't reply, so I suspect I've nailed it. "It's insane. The rumor's insane, and it's even more insane that you would take someone else's word for it. Don't you trust me at all?"

"Well, what am I supposed to think when . . . when you spend all this time with him, and the whole school's going to see you up onstage making out with him?"

"We're not making out! We're pretending! It's called acting! This is so ridiculous. I can't believe we're having an argument about Greg Maxwell. He's not even my type."

This is true. Greg is a nice enough guy, but he's way too into his appearance, has almost nothing to say unless it's written on a script, and wears his khakis so low-slung you can see virtually every inch of his plaid boxer shorts.

"So you're not, like, into him or anything." Hunter sounds sheepish, as he should.

"No, I told you. He's not my type."

"What is your type?" He glances over at me, fishing for compliments.

"Oh, I don't know," I say breezily, gazing out the window at the dirty snow banked up against the sidewalk. "Someone who's five foot eleven, maybe. About a hundred and seventy-five pounds. Blue eyes, brown hair. Tan kind of fading. Drives a Honda Civic. Plays some sport—football, maybe. Thinks he knows everything."

"I see," says Hunter. All the fight's gone out of his voice; he's almost meek now.

"Know anyone who fits that description?" I ask him.

"I might be able to fix you up with someone I know," he jokes, but then he turns serious again. "I'm sorry, Grace. I just don't like the idea of you spending time with another guy, and him touching you, and . . . well, you know."

"But if I become an actress, this is going to happen all the time," I tell him. "You'll have to get used to it."

"I don't know that I'll ever get used to it." He shakes himself, like he's waking up from a dream. "No point in worrying about it now, though. You becoming an actress is still a big 'if.'"

"Thanks." Now it's my turn to feel annoyed with *him*. "That's a really supportive thing to say. What if I said that you becoming a pro football player is still a big if?"

Hunter gives a big sigh. "I didn't mean to offend you. Maybe you will become an actress—I don't know. All I'm saying is, you're in a high school production. That doesn't mean anything in the real world."

"What—and being a Blue Lobster makes you, like, world famous?" I'm so mad now.

"No, but next year I'll be playing for one of the best college offenses in the country," he says, his tone very even, like he's explaining something to a child. "I'll be traveling all over the country, and the pro scouts will be watching me play. Hell, our games will be televised!

Being in a school musical in a crummy town isn't going to get you noticed in Hollywood."

"You know, you can be a real jerk sometimes," I say, my eyes filling with tears. I blink them back and pull my bag onto my lap, ready to spring out of the car as soon as we reach my house.

"I'm just telling you the way things are," he says, looking at me all apologetic. He turns into my driveway and pulls in behind my father's car. "I'm sorry if it dispels your illusions."

"The only illusions I have are the ones about you being a nice guy," I say, heaving myself out of the car and slamming the door behind me. My dramatic departure is spoiled when I slip on some ice and skid toward the front porch, but I don't look back. Maybe my parents are right. I don't know why I'm knocking myself out to make time for Hunter.

Chapter Fourteen

At school the next day, Hunter apologizes and tells me he was completely out of line.

"I'm just jealous of the time you spend away from me," he says, leaning across the lunch table to grasp my hands. The pale blue of his sweater makes his eyes seem even more intense. "That's why I acted so crummy yesterday."

It's impossible not to forgive him, especially when he's looking up at me like a sad puppy. I know my parents think our relationship is kind of volatile, but they don't understand how much Hunter and I care about each other. To them, he's just the confident, good-looking guy who comes over to pick me up. They think we don't have anything in common because he's a football player and I'm a drama club geek. They don't see how vulnerable he can be, how insecure he can get, even though he's a big hero at school.

I wriggle a hand free and blow him a kiss across the table, to show that everything's fine again.

"You know, I e-mailed Miss Sara to tell her about the show," I say.

"Who?"

"You remember—my singing teacher from camp. I don't think I would have gotten the part without her. She really boosted my confidence."

"So, what'd she say?"

"That's the weird thing," I tell him. "It's been weeks, but I haven't heard back from her. I thought she'd be really excited."

"Maybe she's busy." Hunter shrugs. "Maybe she doesn't check her e-mail very often. Lots of old people only look at it, like, once a month."

"She's not *that* old. Maybe she is just really busy right now. Do you think I should e-mail her again?"

But Hunter is distracted by one of his Blue Lobster buddies shouting to him from the other side of the cafeteria, and he doesn't answer me.

If February and March are all about rehearsals, April is all about showtime. We've learned our lines, sung all our numbers dozens of times, practiced our dance steps, been fitted for costumes, and, in the two weeks before the show, gone to rehearsal every single day after school. I've rehearsed with the whole cast, with the Pink Ladies, alone with Greg, alone with Terri, and alone with Wei, the girl playing Frenchy. At first I wasn't sure which of these experiences was worse: being stared at and judged by the whole cast, or feeling utterly exposed in a more intimate situation. Rehearsals with Terri were especially difficult, because—as she whispered to me one day—her intention was to act me off the stage. Sometimes this seemed to mean actually *pushing* me off the stage. Mrs. Lane had to keep reminding Terri to hit her marks without blocking me from the audience or shoving me into the wings.

On the Thursday afternoon before the show begins, Nick Smart arrives late to rehearsals. We're all doing the big high school dance production number onstage, trying it out with the school orchestra for only the second time, and it's not going well. The dancing is all out of time and still kind of tentative, to Ms. Schaeffer's despair. The band keeps drowning out the lines of dialogue. One of Terri's friends, Penelope Smith, is playing Cha-Cha, the slutty girl from St. Bernadette's who takes over Sandy's spot with Danny during the dance. Penelope's supposed to twirl me away so she can take my place next to Greg Maxwell, but instead she grabs my wrist so hard she practically dislocates it, sending me staggering into another dancing couple. All three of us collapse in a heap and bring the scene to yet another halt. Mrs. Lane has her head in her hands when Nick Smart strolls in.

She and Nick have a quick conference with Ms.

Schaeffer and Mr. Hall, the music teacher who's conducting the orchestra. We all stand around on the stage, whispering and nudging each other, people gossiping about what Nick's wearing (one of those sheepskin flight jackets, to go with the aviator sunglasses he took off when he walked in) or how Ms. Schaeffer keeps flicking her hair and laughing in an obvious way every time he looks at her. Then the huddle of adults breaks up, and Nick pulls off his jacket and drapes it over the back of a seat.

"Okay, everyone," he calls. "Here's what we're going to do. First, I want the band to sit this one out. Everyone onstage—I want to see all your dance steps without music. Susie—I mean, Ms. Schaeffer—will count out your steps."

Ms. Schaeffer beams at him and picks up the megaphone.

"Then, band—we'll play through this part of the score with everyone standing still onstage," says Nick, with his hands on his hips. "The principals with dialogue will say their lines, and we'll work on the volume balance. Then we'll put it all together. Everyone can stay late tonight, right? It's now or never. Once you're up onstage with an audience watching you, you don't get a second chance. Okay, Susie. Over to you."

There's something about Nick Smart's presence that makes everyone try extra hard. I forget about my throbbing wrist, and the way that Greg and I still can't manage to dance in unison, and just throw myself into the scene. A performer lives in the moment, Miss Sara always said, so I really try to overcome my anxieties and bumble my way through. We finish rehearsal that night more than forty minutes late, so late that numerous annoyed or worried parents, tired of sitting in their cold cars, sneak into the auditorium to watch. When Nick finally raises his hand and shouts "Okay—you can go!" everyone is completely exhausted. But it was worth it: the number has really come together, and for the first time it feels like we actually have a show. Even Mrs. Lane is smiling.

My brother is leaning against the wall, waiting for me to climb down from the stage, jingling the car keys at me to get my attention.

"Did you see much of it?" I ask him, dragging on my coat and groping in my bag for my umbrella.

"See it? I feel like I could do it myself by now," he says in mock-complaint. "That Nick Smart dude sure thinks he's hot stuff."

"Isn't he great?"

"Whatever. I bet he has leg warmers on under those jeans. Doesn't Emily want a ride?"

"Maybe." I swing around to look for Emily. She's with a bunch of other girls, heading out the far door. "Hey, Em! Want a ride?"

"It's okay!" she calls over her shoulder, and disappears through the door.

"What's the deal with her?" Tom asks, waiting for me to pick up my backpack.

"Nothing," I say, and then I hesitate. There's nothing *wrong* between me and Emily: it's just that she has a lot of new friends now, and I guess I do, too. Well, I have Hunter, and he has a lot of friends. That's almost the same thing.

"Let's go, Gracie." Tom claps a hand on my shoulder and steers me to the door. "Unless you want to go kiss your guru Nick Smart good-bye."

"Shut up!" I hiss at him, but I don't think anyone heard. There's nobody anywhere near me. Everyone else has left already, or is standing around talking to their friends. I'm the only one who's not part of a crowd.

At last it's the Tuesday we've all been waiting for—opening night. I have to be back at school by six in order to get ready. My whole family is coming tonight, and my parents have bought tickets for Saturday night as well. In fact, there'll be di Giovanni family members at every performance, because my father has browbeaten all our relatives into buying tickets. He's also managed to persuade most of his patients to attend. He's so shameless: he even called the school to see if he could sell tickets at his office, to make sure his patients couldn't wriggle out of buying them.

"Your grandmother called to tell you to break an arm," my mother says, kissing me good-bye and handing me a clutch of hangers bearing my plastic-covered costumes. "She gets confused sometimes."

"Thanks, Ma," I say, my voice all wavery. I feel sick to my stomach. I'm sure I *will* break something tonight, like my ankle when I trip offstage, or a piece of scenery when I crash into it, or Mrs. Lane's heart when I stand there in the spotlight, frozen like a deer in headlights, unable to remember a single line.

"You're going to do just fine," she says. "You know this part back to front and inside out."

"*She* knows it!" sniffs Sonia, on her way up to shower and get ready. "We all know it. When this show is over, I plan to use that particular CD as a Frisbee."

"Bye, Rascal," I say, bending down to pat the dog good-bye. He wags his tail. I wish I were staying at home with him tonight instead of going out in the rain to make a fool of myself in public. What on earth made me think I could do this?

"Come on, Grace," says my father, who's driving me over to school and then rushing home to get ready himself. "Your adoring public awaits."

"That's what I'm afraid of," I mutter, following him out the front door.

Backstage, it's a mob scene. The rooms we're using to get changed reek of greasy cosmetics, hair spray, and sweat. The girls' room is clogged with tables, mirrors, and clothes rails on wheels for our costumes. Every step I take is potentially lethal, because the floor is littered with shoes, discarded nylons, dropped ribbons, and plugged-in hair dryers. Three mothers have volunteered to oversee our makeup and hairdos, and one of them helps me sweep my hair up into a high, bouncy ponytail, securing a scarf around it with clips. Every so often there's a shriek because someone's burned her hair, or got chewing gum stuck to her earrings. Mrs. Lane appears behind me, looking like she's had way too much coffee.

"Let's see you, Grace," she says, spinning me around. I'm wearing a swirly pink skirt, a white blouse and belt, a pale pink cardigan with one button fastened, and flat ballet pumps. "You look just perfect. Now remember, in the opening number, keep your head up and watch for your mark stage left."

I don't know how I'm supposed to keep my head up AND look for my mark, but I nod, and Mrs. Lane rushes away to give out more instructions. Emily appears on the other side of the mirror, dressed just like me, except her skirt and cardigan are pale blue. We look at each other and burst out laughing—we both have *so* much stage makeup on, our faces are almost clownlike.

"Look at us, G!" Emily says, standing close to me and gazing at our reflection in the mirror. "We look totally prim. Audrey would be so proud."

"Apart from the makeup," I say. "Audrey might think it's a little much."

"I don't know—I think I look kind of hot," Emily jokes. "Damn, is that the orchestra warming up already?"

"Ladies of the chorus!" shrieks Ms. Schaeffer, who's standing on a chair by the door, brandishing a clipboard. She's dressed in black leggings and a turtleneck tonight so she can't be spotted lurking in the wings. "It's time to take your positions. Big smiles, everyone!"

"Is Nick Smart here?" Penelope asks, and Ms. Schaeffer frowns at her. Nick Smart is her property, apparently.

"Shhh . . . no more talking, now. Total silence once you leave this room!"

"But—"

"Save it for the performance," snaps Ms. Schaeffer, and with that, the room empties.

Terri, wearing a tight black pencil skirt and satin bomber jacket, is the last one out the door before me. She pauses abruptly and glances back over her shoulder.

"Hey," she says, looking me up and down with tight-lipped disapproval. "Try not to mess things up. I don't want you making everyone else look like amateurs just because you are, okay?"

I open my mouth to respond. But then a sudden calm descends on me. I decide to take Ms. Schaeffer's advice and save it for the performance. I don't want to waste my voice squabbling with Terri. It's showtime, and no matter what, the big opening number is still mine.

Chapter Fifteen

The show is a big success, sold out for all of its five nights. We have a few rocky moments—people missing their cues, some technical glitches with lights and props, especially during the simulation of the big car race, and one minor accident when one of the guys takes too big a step during a dance routine and ends up tumbling off a bleacher and falling flat on his butt. But despite all my anxieties—and Terri's warning—I manage to keep it together. In fact, I do more than that. Every night up there onstage, I sing and dance my heart out. With each performance, I feel myself getting stronger and more confident. By Saturday night, I've lost almost any shred of self-consciousness. It's like every part of me has relaxed, and I can really throw myself into the role.

When the spotlight's shining in my eyes, and all I can make out beyond the orchestra is a ghostly mass of faces in the dark, all looking up at me, I don't feel nervous and uncertain anymore. Sure, my heart is still beating fast, but it's more of an electric thrill rather than blind panic. And when I finish a solo number and pause for a moment, trying to catch my breath before the music starts again, it's the best feeling in the world. I listen to the thunderous applause, the whoops and hollers rising up from the audience, and it's hard to process the idea that they're all applauding *me*. Hunter's out there, and so are my parents and my brother and sister, and I know they're cheering for me, but most of the audience are total strangers. This is what I've always wanted to do, but until now I didn't really believe it was possible. I didn't really believe I could do it.

Nick Smart *is* there on opening night, though hardly anybody sees him—we're all too flustered—and he leaves Mrs. Lane a set of notes, things he wants us to fix before the next performance. He's back again on Friday and Saturday, everywhere at once: in the guys' dressing room, giving them a preshow pep talk; in the wings helping the stage manager get people on and off; at the back of the hall, he tells us later, just watching and enjoying the show. On Saturday night, when I'm on my way back to the dressing room during intermission to get changed into my second-act costume, he startles me by taking hold of my arm. I hadn't even noticed him in the throng of people.

"Grace," he says as I clumsily reel toward him. "You got a second?"

My heart starts thudding. I nod and step out of the way of everyone else stampeding to the dressing rooms. Nick looks really serious, his eyebrows knitted together. I so hope I haven't done anything wrong.

"I just wanted to tell you something," he says, lowering his voice. I grit my teeth and prepare for the worst. "You're a star."

I don't know what to say to this, so I just stand there, probably looking stupid, feeling my face get hotter and hotter.

"You've got a really expressive face and singing voice, and boy, are you working them both! You did a great job in rehearsals, but up there on the stage—well, you just come alive. You have the audience eating out of your hand, you know that?"

I shake my head. I feel like bursting into tears— from relief, from pride, from sheer exhaustion at this point.

"So go get changed, and remember, it's not over yet." He gives my arm a quick squeeze. "Final act, I want you to knock it out of the park, okay?"

I start nodding again, like one of those goofy little bobblehead dolls you see in the back window of a car, and Nick heads off toward the stage door. My feet feel glued to the floor, but inside I'm leaping for joy. Nick

Smart thinks I'm a star! This is possibly the best moment of my life, ever.

"Grace!" Ms. Schaeffer sweeps up, her eyes bulging out of her head. This week has pushed her from over-the-top peppiness into nervous breakdown territory. "Why are you dawdling out here? You're the star of the show, for God's sake! You need to get changed—go, go, go!"

The star of the show. Me, Grace di Giovanni. Can my life get any better—or any weirder—than this?

When the final curtain comes down that night, we've all sung ourselves hoarse, bowed so often that we're all dizzy, and danced so much we've got blisters on top of blisters. And just like that, it's all over. In the girls' room, cast members are crying and hugging each other, reluctant to take off their costumes and clean off their makeup because it's the last night. Even Mrs. Lane looks emotional, coming in to congratulate us and telling us to hurry up and get ready for the after-party in the staff room. As for Ms. Schaeffer, she's a total wreck. She's slumped weeping in a chair while girls try to calm her down by fanning her with programs.

"You were all so wonderful," she sobs. "*This* was all so wonderful!"

"She's like this after the cheerleading regionals too," Penelope Smith mutters.

After I clean off my thick, sweat-streaked makeup, I start wriggling out of my skintight final costume—black vinyl pants and bustier—and kick off my high-heeled black shoes.

"G!" Emily appears at my side, already changed into jeans and a pretty embroidered top. "Don't take that off—wear it to the party!"

"Yeah!" chorus the girls around me, all telling me how cute I look.

"Really?" I'm doubtful. Normally I would never wear something as way-out as this.

"Dude, you look hot," Emily insists. "And when else will you get the chance to parade around a party looking like a prostitute without your parents throwing a fit?"

So I take her advice and just finish cleaning my face before heading to the after-party, trailing after Emily and her gang. When I enter the staff room—festooned with one of Ms. Schaeffer's trademark banners, announcing GREASE IS THE WORD!! in giant glittery letters—people start clapping and wolf-whistling. I can't help blushing at all the attention. Terri Cooper rolls her eyes at me, but I notice she's still wearing part of *her* costume as well—Rizzo's tight black pencil skirt.

The noise level is intense because everyone's talking and squealing and letting loose after all the tension of the past few months. The boys have the food table pretty much surrounded and are stuffing their faces like they haven't eaten in days. Though the party is supposed to be for cast and teachers only, plus special guests like the mayor and Nick Smart, I see that several of the Blue Lobsters are there, swanning around the room, chatting up girls and helping themselves to free food. Just then, I feel a hand on the small of my back, and suddenly I'm in Hunter's arms.

"I'm so proud of you," he murmurs, pulling me close. I turn to mush inside whenever he holds me like this. It's like everyone else in the room disappears. "You were just unbelievable up there."

"Thanks," I whisper. I close my eyes and breathe in his clean, musky smell. Sometimes I feel like I'm almost addicted to it. Then I hear Principal Thomas trying to get everyone's attention so he can make a speech, and I open my eyes. Hunter is frowning at me, eyeing me up and down.

"Why didn't you get changed like everyone else?" he asks me in a low, strained voice.

"What . . . why?" I'm confused. People are clapping because of something Mr. Thomas just said, but I missed it.

"You look kind of slutty," Hunter mutters, staring down at my pointy shoes. "Everyone's staring at you."

"Everyone was staring at me onstage," I say as quietly as I can, because people are starting to look at us.

"That's different," he says.

I shake my head at him and try to concentrate on what Mr. Thomas is saying. Why is Hunter trying to spoil things? This is the greatest night of my life so far, and he's acting all annoyed at me. If he weren't a Blue Lobster, he wouldn't have even been allowed in the room. And just for a second, I wish he hadn't been— allowed in, that is. If all he's going to do is make me feel small, then maybe he should have just gone home with the rest of the audience.

Mr. Thomas introduces Mrs. Lane, and she talks about how proud she is of all of us. I'm still fuming about Hunter's comments—it's like my head is cloudy. I felt so great when I first walked in the room. Now I feel self-conscious again, wondering if he's right. Maybe I should have changed into my jeans and a T-shirt so I wouldn't stand out so much. Maybe everyone else is thinking how conceited I am, keeping my costume on like this. My bare shoulders feel exposed, and because of my high heels, I seem to tower over everybody else in the room.

Now Nick Smart steps up to offer a few remarks, talking about how this is a great night for Cumberland High, and how many Broadway theaters would be happy to have a cast as good as ours. This drives everyone wild, of course, and in all the chaos of screaming and clapping and jumping up and down, some of the Blue Lobsters manage to make out with various chorus girls without any teachers noticing.

"And I want to thank two people in particular," Nick says, when the cheering dies down. "Come up here, Greg and Grace."

I move away from Hunter and, head down, work my way through the crowd. Greg is already standing next to Nick when I reach them, a huge smile on his face. He's wearing his KISS ME, I'M FAMOUS! T-shirt and his lucky black plaid boxers, three inches of which are visible above the drooping waistband of his jeans.

"Here she is," says Nick, taking my hand. I turn to face the room, suddenly feeling intensely shy. "Ladies and gentlemen, let's hear it for your truly amazing leads."

More screaming and craziness now—so much that I almost burst out laughing. But then I see Hunter staring at me, looking incredibly pissed off. I guess it's because Nick is still holding my hand, so I tug my hand free and nervously adjust my top, pulling it up a little higher.

"And now," shouts Nick, "it's time to party like it's 1959!"

Mr. Fisher starts hammering away on the piano like

170

his life depends on it, and I gaze around the room. Everyone looks like they're fizzing with happiness. I can see Emily chatting a mile a minute to a group of girls, and they're all pink-cheeked and laughing, hugging each other. Someone hands me a plastic cup of something warm, fizzy, and—as I discover when I take a sip—entirely nonalcoholic, and I try to get back in the party mood again.

But really what I feel right now is tired, dead tired. Maybe this is what all actors feel when a show's run is over: a sense of deflation, of regret, and relief as well. I cling to my drink and lean against the wall, smiling and saying hi to people as they pass. That's about all I'm capable of, I think. Hunter's still over in the corner talking to another Blue Lobster, shooting me looks every minute or so. I feel like he's checking up on me, like he's my bodyguard rather than my boyfriend. Lots of girls would kill for a boyfriend like Hunter. But sometimes it feels as though he's less worried about *me* and more concerned with keeping everyone else away, like he's protecting something that belongs to him.

"Good job, Grace," says Greg, who's being pulled across the room by a very determined member of the Pink Ladies. He pauses to give me a quick hug. "You were great tonight."

"Thanks—you too!" I call as he floats away through the crowd. Hunter has stopped talking and is giving

171

Greg a long, sour stare. Greg is oblivious, luckily; he's preoccupied with signing programs for the Pink Lady's simpering friends, and with kissing them all afterward. But I see the look on Hunter's face, and I don't like it. I don't like the way it makes me feel.

Chapter Sixteen

The show has been so all consuming this semester, it's hard to get back into the routine of regular school again. A week after the final performance, it almost feels like the last few months were all a dream. True, I know more people now, and more people know me. Someone will say hi to me in the hallway, and I'll have no idea who they are; some of the younger kids at school whisper and nudge each other when I walk by. It's fame on a totally minor scale, and it probably won't last very long.

Cumberland High is already preoccupied with another group of Blue Lobsters—this time the baseball team, known as the Blue Lobster Diamonds or the BLDs—especially now that Ms. Schaeffer has turned in her black turtleneck and clipboard. She and her band of superseniors are hard at work on preparations for the Diamond Nights Dance. That's our version of prom, except it's open to everyone in the school—

which means it's pretty lame and boycotted by most of the A-listers.

Hunter has a few days off from school to fly out to Michigan—all expenses paid—and meet his future coach and teammates. He's way excited about the trip, and I'm really happy for him. It's true that he was kind of annoying and possessive at the closing-night party, but he was just feeling a little neglected after weeks of intensive rehearsals and performances. Now that the show's over, everything is completely fine between us again. Every relationship has its ups and downs. And despite all the pressures of schoolwork, I have plenty of time to see him on weekends.

While he's away, I have to eat lunch by myself every day. Although people do recognize me and say hello to me and all, I didn't really make any close friends in the show. And nowadays, Emily is busier than ever. Not only does she have some vast crowd of brand new buddies, she's really getting into this whole photography thing. After one day of sitting by myself in the cafeteria, feeling kind of forlorn, I ask her after the last class of the morning if she's doing anything at lunchtime.

"We're going to Photoshop some of the shots I took at this weekend's game," she tells me. "Jason wants to do a whole spread on the BLDs."

Jason is the editor of the school newspaper, and one

of the linchpins of Emily's new circle. I'd say she has a crush on him, but he's a geeky short guy who squints, and laughs like a seal.

"That's great," I say, though my heart is sinking at the prospect of eating alone again. "How about tomorrow?"

"We're having an editorial meeting."

"Really?" I feel my face droop. "You have to do newspaper things two days running?"

"Three, actually." Emily swings her bag onto her shoulder and checks her watch. We're the last two people left in the classroom. "You know, the spring special issue is coming up."

"Oh," I say. "I see. It's just . . ." My voice trails away. I don't want to sound like a loser.

"What?" says Emily, kind of impatiently. "It's just that Hunter's away, and you don't want to sit by yourself at lunchtime?"

"Well . . . yeah."

"Thanks, G. No, really, I mean it." She rolls her eyes, annoyed. "I'm glad you think of me as a stand-in for when Hunter's not here. Sort of a second-string quarterback, right?"

"I didn't mean it like that," I protest.

"Look, I've got to go," says Emily, and then she lowers her voice and looks me in the eye. "I'm sorry that you have to eat by yourself, but that's not my fault, is it? You're the one who wants it to be all Hunter, all the time. Did you ever think that some days *I* have to eat lunch by myself because you're all wrapped up with lover boy?"

"I thought you'd made all these new friends," I argue.

"Yeah, well, I had to," she says. "You've been kind of unavailable, you know."

"I'm free right now," I say with a hopeful shrug. But right away I realize this is the wrong thing to say.

"Not everything revolves around you, Grace," says Emily, her expression cold. "I've got my own stuff going on right now. And let's face it, in a couple of days, when Hunter's back, you won't care whether I'm busy or not. You won't even give me a second's thought."

"That's not true!"

"Isn't it? Ask yourself this—when was the last time you asked me over just to hang out? When was the last time you called me without wanting to talk about your part in the show or what's going on with you and Hunter?"

"But that's what's going on in my life right now," I say, trying to defend myself.

"Exactly. *Your* life, not mine." Emily checks her watch again. "Did you ever think that maybe I had things I was stressing over, too? Things I wanted to talk about?"

"You know you can talk about anything with me!"

"You mean I *used* to be able to talk about anything with you. Now you're just obsessed with your own fabulous life. Remember last year when we had our Audrey Hepburn movie marathon for my birthday? We planned it for weeks. I don't even think you know when my birthday is anymore."

"Of course I do!" Now I'm in a panic. Did I miss Emily's birthday? What's the date today? "It's . . . it's at the end of this month, right?"

"Whatever," she says, shaking her head. "Look, really, I have to go—I'm late already."

She zooms off out the door and down the hallway without a backward glance.

I had no idea that Emily was so annoyed with me. It's not fair—she was the one who wanted me to get the lead, and she was the one encouraging me to go out with Hunter. Suddenly, because all our plans for this year have worked out, I'm the selfish one.

I get in the cafeteria line feeling completely gloomy, and by the time I pay for my plate of limp salad and a lukewarm dollop of macaroni and cheese, I feel even worse. Guilty, even. Emily's right, in a way. When I sit with Hunter at lunchtime at our usual table in the corner, I'm preoccupied with him. I don't *see* anyone else half the time. If Emily were sitting somewhere by herself, I probably wouldn't notice. But she's wrong in thinking this means I'm selfish. I never meant to drive her away or make her feel out of it; I genuinely thought she had other things to do and people to see.

"Eating alone today, Grace?" says a sly voice behind me. Great—it's Terri Cooper, nudging me with her tray of food.

"I guess," I say, trying to sound unconcerned, like it hadn't occurred to me until this minute.

"I'd ask you to sit with me," she says, "but our table is already full."

I grimace and hand over my money to the cashier, holding my hand out for the change. The quicker I can get away from Terri, the better.

"It's hard, isn't it?" She gives a theatrical sigh. "Now the show's over, you're back to being a nobody. But you're used to that, aren't you?"

"Whatever," I say, picking up my tray and stalking away from her with as much dignity as I can muster. I gaze around the room looking for somewhere to sit, or for anyone I know, but suddenly the cafeteria seems very full and very unfriendly. All the drama club people I recognize are at full tables, and none of them are exactly waving me over. And the Blue Lobsters who are always calling out to Hunter or dropping by our table are ignoring me. Without Hunter, it's like I'm invisible.

Finally I spot an empty seat at the end of a long table. It's an otherwise all-boy table—boys who are still so young they're flicking food at each other and arguing about Dungeons & Dragons. When I sit down, they stop talking for a moment and stare at me. Then one squirts some ketchup at the kid opposite, and they all start sniggering. I stare down at my plate and eat my lunch without looking up. I can't bear to see Terri and her friends laughing at me.

When I get home from school, my mother calls to me from the living room. I leave my bag in the hall and flop into an armchair.

"I just got off the phone with the director from your summer camp." My mother accidentally drops her address book onto Rascal's recumbent form at her feet. He doesn't even seem to notice. "I called to tell her about you doing so well in the show. Then I remembered that she was a Georgetown grad. What a coincidence!"

Sonia just heard that she got into Georgetown, her first choice for college. My parents are insane with happiness about it, though they show it in different ways: my mother is calling everyone she's ever met in her entire life, whether they know Sonia or not, and my father is complaining about how it's going to bankrupt him. This is a joke, because Sonia's also won some big scholarship. We're all really proud of her, though I think it's hard for Tom right now—he's already had rejection letters from his number one and two choices, and Sonia's success just makes him feel like even more of a loser.

"Really." I'm still thinking about my depressing day at school. Emily didn't even sit next to me in class this afternoon. I feel like a total social pariah. My mother keeps talking, but I'm not really paying attention.

". . . about your singing teacher, Miss Sara," my mother is saying.

"What about Miss Sara, Ma?"

"Well, apparently she's quite ill. She had a heart attack and has been housebound for some time, but last week she was taken to the hospital."

"No!" I gasp. No wonder I never heard back from Miss Sara. "Can we go see her?"

"I'm not even sure which hospital she's in, Grace. Somewhere in upstate New York, I guess. I could try to find out, but you know, honey, maybe the family wouldn't want a lot of kids from the summer camp turning up."

"I'm not 'a lot of kids'—I'm just me."

"I know, I know," says my mother. "But maybe you should just write her a letter or a card. . . . Hang on."

The phone is ringing again, and my mother picks up.

It's one of my ten million cousins, apparently calling to talk about how Sonia is a genius who brings honor to the entire family. This is my mother's favorite topic, so it looks like she'll be on the phone for a long time. I slouch off up to my room and close the door, wondering about Miss Sara. I hope she's not really sick. Tomorrow after school I'll buy her a card and ask my mother to find out where to send it—if she can manage to stop talking about Sonia for two minutes.

At dinner, my mother spends half the meal reciting the litany of compliments she's received about Sonia's success.

"Auntie Lena said she never had a second's doubt that you'd get in," she tells Sonia. "And Auntie Trini said that she had told a neighbor that you had applied to Georgetown, and this person said she knew someone who used to go to Georgetown, and they said it was one of the best schools in the country and that only the cream of the crop get in, and Auntie Trini told them that you are the cream of the crop, and she wasn't just saying that because you're her great-niece. And now she's been proved right, and she can't wait to see that person again so she can put them straight."

"Ma," pleads Sonia. "Please stop telling everyone. It's not such a big deal. Can we talk about something else for a change?"

She glances at Tom and frowns, no doubt hoping my parents will notice how upset he looks. "Grace, how was *your* day?"

I know Sonia's trying to make Tom feel better, so I try to think of something to say other than "It sucked."

"Um," I falter. "Well, I . . . I heard from Emily that the school newspaper is going to put out a special issue."

Sonia gives me a can't-you-do-better-than-that? look.

"About baseball," I continue, trying—and failing—to sound enthusiastic.

Tom throws down his fork. "Well, I've got some news," he announces, staring around the table at all of us. "I got another college rejection today."

Both my parents look pained.

"Oh, Tom," says my mother. "Why didn't you say something earlier? Which college?"

"What does it matter?" he demands, folding his arms. "It's third time unlucky."

"You're still waiting on another one, right?" asks Sonia sympathetically.

"Maybe that'll work out," I add. I feel so bad for my brother.

"Maybe. Maybe not."

"It's a setback," says my father. He looks very

182

glum, cutting up his chicken without much enthusiasm. "But there are always other options."

"What? Like community college?" Tom is all angry and defiant. "Yeah, right. I'd rather go back into construction again."

"There's nothing wrong with community college." Oh, no. Here we go. My father is getting red in the face. "It's better than no college at all."

"Maybe you can apply to some more places," says my mother.

"Maybe you can all get off my back for one minute," says Tom. He's so hotheaded, I wish he would just calm down. "Why can't you just accept that Sonia's the smart one, I'm the dumb one, and I'm never going to get into any college?"

"You're not dumb—you're just lazy!" snaps my father. "Sonia worked hard, but you blew off your SAT. You always think you know better than everyone else!"

"Now, now," says my mother, desperate to make peace, as ever. "We should talk about this later, when we're not so upset, maybe—"

"There's nothing to talk about!" Tom pushes back from the table. "This affects me, not you. Why don't you just go back to being happy about Sonia and leave me alone?"

"Because you're a member of this family, whether

183

you like it or not!" shouts my father. Just then, the phone starts ringing, though you can barely hear it with everyone shouting.

"I'll get it," I mumble, and wriggle out of my seat—any excuse to get out of there. I grab the phone and head into the living room, a finger in one ear to block out all the noise. "Hello?"

"Grace, is that you?" It's a man's voice, but I can't place it at first. One of my uncles, probably, calling to pay homage to Sonia.

"Yes, it's me."

"Grace, this is Nick Smart." Nick Smart! This must be some kind of joke. Why would Nick Smart be calling me? "Mrs. Lane gave me your number—I wanted to speak to you right away. There's an audition coming up for a new Broadway musical based on *Anne of Green Gables,* and they've already got Joanna Carlton playing the lead—you know, the girl from that Disney show."

"Sure," I say, still in a total daze.

"But there are several smaller roles for girls, and I think you should audition for one. They're having an open casting call in two weeks. You'd have to take an afternoon off from school, but Mrs. Lane said that wouldn't be a problem."

"No," I say. "I mean, yes, it'll be fine."

"It'll be at the Pavilion Theater on West Forty-fourth

Street," he says. "I'll get the rest of the details and e-mail them to Mrs. Lane, okay?"

When I put down the phone, everyone at the table is still arguing, so I can escape upstairs without anyone even noticing. I can't believe it: Nick Smart wants me to audition for an actual Broadway show!

Chapter Seventeen

This is incredibly exciting news for me, but I decide to keep it to myself. Now's not really the best time to discuss anything with my parents; the argument with Tom seems to go on all evening. Hunter sends me a sweet text message just before I go to bed, to say he's having a great time in Michigan and thinking of me, but I resist the urge to write to him about the call. Something tells me he might not like the idea of Nick Smart calling me at home. And after the things Emily said to me about only contacting her to talk about myself . . . well, I guess that means I should think twice before picking up the phone in general.

The next day at school, I hunt down Mrs. Lane, and she gives me the information I need.

"This is an incredible experience for you, Grace," she tells me, searching through the mess on her desk for the relevant piece of paper. "A lot of the other girls auditioning will be professional actresses with agents.

Nick must really think highly of you if he thinks you should try out."

This makes me feel incredibly nervous. I hadn't even thought of that—that the other girls will be real actresses who go to theater schools and appear in commercials and stuff like that. Suddenly the audition doesn't seem quite so exciting. It just feels daunting.

"Even if nothing comes of it, you mustn't be put off," Mrs. Lane says, like she's reading my mind. She gives me a kind smile. "Don't look so terrified!"

"But I can't compete with real actresses," I tell her.

"There's no such thing as a *real* actress," says Mrs. Lane, her lips twitching into a wry smile. "There are just good and bad ones. And if Nick Smart thinks you're a good one, then you should take that as a very great compliment."

"Do you really think I've got a chance of getting a part?" I ask her.

"If you didn't have a chance, Nick wouldn't be suggesting this," she says. "But remember, Grace, this is an open casting call. You don't know what the producers are looking for, or how many other girls are going to show up. And very few unknowns step off the street and straight into a Broadway musical. You shouldn't be unrealistic about this."

"Then why should I even bother to audition?" I feel even more daunted now.

"All actresses have to go through a lot of rejection and disappointment. It's part of the process. You need to develop a thick skin, and going to this audition is the first step. It's an experience you need to have."

"My first real audition," I muse.

"The first of many, I hope," says Mrs. Lane, handing me the directions to the theater. "What do your parents think about this?"

"Oh, they're really pleased," I say quickly. There's no point in revealing that I haven't told them yet.

"Will your mother go with you to the audition?"

"Yeah . . . probably. If she has time, I mean."

"Well, let me know if you need any more information," says Mrs. Lane, distracted by a pile of papers about to slide off her desk. "And don't forget to rehearse your audition piece, okay?"

I fold the directions, shove them into my bag, and scurry away to my next class.

That evening, I wait until dinner to tell my parents. Tom is coming home late tonight because he's got the final track meet of the school year coming up and has to practice, so this means we'll have a relatively tension-free mealtime for a change. Also, I want to tell my parents when Sonia is there. Since she got the news about Georgetown, she's been in the best possible mood; she can back me up if they have any objections.

I figure they'll be surprised and maybe a little wary about my going into the city for this audition. But I never imagined they'd think the whole thing was a bad idea.

"I don't know, Grace," says my mother, shaking her head. This is her typical way of saying no. "It's too soon to start thinking this big. Being in the school play is one thing, but Broadway? It's too much for you to take on."

"I'm not taking anything on! I'm just going to an audition!"

"You'll have to take a day off from school," objects my father. "Haven't you got tests coming up? You don't want to mess up your education, like your brother is intent on doing, just to run after some crazy dream."

"It's not a crazy dream," I say, totally miserable at their reaction. "Nick Smart thinks I can do this."

"God, not him again." Sonia rolls her eyes. *Thanks, Sonia!* "I thought we'd heard the last of him for a while. He's just some short guy who couldn't make it as an actor."

"He's a director," I snap at her. "He won a Tony!"

"Who hasn't?" Sonia shrugs and leans over me to pick up the salt. I feel like biting her arm.

"Grace, it would be one thing if school was over for the year," says my mother. "And this semester has been so crazy for you already with the show. Really, it's just

189

too much pressure. Your father is right, you need to focus on your schoolwork. You're going to be applying to colleges soon. . . ."

"In the fall!" I protest.

"And what happens if you get this part?" asks my father. "The school show took up so much time. This would be even worse. You'd probably have to drop out of school."

"Don't be ridiculous, Dad—of course I wouldn't drop out of school! Anyway, Mrs. Lane said my chances of getting a part are really slim."

"Then why bother?" sniffs Sonia.

"This is all about getting experience at a serious audition," I say, really desperate now. I've forgotten all my fears about going. At this point, I don't mind if they laugh me off the stage of the Pavilion Theater. I just want this opportunity. "This is the kind of experience I need if I'm going to become an actress."

My parents exchange looks—the kind that means they think I'm talking like a crazy person. When is my family going to take me seriously?

"Listen, Gracie, every girl wants to become an actress at some point," Sonia lectures me in her most patronizing older-sister voice. "Then we grow up and get real."

"Just because you gave up doesn't mean I'm going to!" I remember that Sonia dropped out of the drama club a couple of years ago, probably when she realized she was never going to get a lead role. "This is really important to me."

"Getting the part in *Grease* has totally gone to her head," Sonia says, addressing my parents as though I'm not there.

My mother hushes her. "There's plenty of time for you to audition and get experience," she says, patting my hand. "You're only sixteen. There's no big hurry."

"Honey, we're just thinking about your best interests," says my father, breaking a piece of bread in two. "These people in the city are sharks. They'll eat you up and spit you out."

"It's not going to be like the nice supportive atmosphere at school," agrees my mother.

If my parents really think that school is a "nice supportive" place, they're the crazy ones.

"You'll be a total wreck for weeks," predicts Sonia. "You'll be weeping all over the house."

"You're just not tough enough yet," my mother says. "I know you, Grace. You're going to give it your all and really get your hopes up. Then you'll be crushed when nothing comes of it. It's just not worth it."

"Well, I think it is," I say, choking back tears of utter frustration. I don't want to cry in front of them and prove Sonia right.

* * *

Hunter is finally back from Michigan. The weather is beautiful, so we drive out to Belvedere Point and go for a walk along the beach. Hunter has tons to tell me about the University of Michigan, about its gorgeous campus, and how amazing the sports facilities are there. And he thinks I'd really like Ann Arbor, with all its cafés and bookstores. He's already got everything worked out—how I'll visit him every couple of months next year, how I can go away with him and his buddies next spring break.

He's forgotten one really important thing, of course: my parents. If they freak out at the idea of my catching a train into the city to go to an audition for a couple of hours, the chances of them letting me fly halfway across the country to stay with Hunter in a college dorm are extremely remote. Though they haven't said anything more about me and Hunter seeing less of each other, I suspect they were hoping that things would cool off between us during all the show rehearsals and per-formances. That didn't happen, of course, but maybe now they're thinking that it'll all come to a natural end when Hunter goes away to college in August. Every so often my mother makes really loaded comments that are supposed to be offhand, like, "You don't have to get too serious, you know—there are plenty of other fish in the sea."

Sometimes our relationship *does* feel a little bit too intense. After the sun sets, we sit in the car looking out over Belvedere Point. I really like kissing and snuggling with Hunter—it makes me feel so safe and happy. But tonight he seems kind of agitated, and it feels like he's all over me. I want to talk, to tell him about this whole audition thing, and I have to push him away so I can say my piece.

"So they just point-blank refused to consider it," I complain after telling him about the disastrous dinner-table conversation. "Can you believe it?"

Hunter gives a big sigh and stares out at the sea. "Well, you know, maybe your parents are right about this," he says at last.

"What?"

"I mean, the school show is just over, and that was bad enough." He has his arm around my shoulders still, and he tugs at me, trying to pull me closer. "This would take up *all* your time."

"If I got a part—probably," I admit.

"You know, it's only a few months before I head off," he says. "It would really suck if you had rehearsals and stuff all summer. I'd never get to see my baby at all."

He presses a kiss onto the crown of my head.

"But it's unlikely I'll get beyond the first audition," I explain. "I don't have any experience or anything."

"It sounds like a lot of stress for nothing," he says.

"Why drive yourself crazy with it when you could be spending time with me? We're going to have a great summer together. I don't want anything to spoil it."

I open my mouth to try and explain some more, but before I can say anything, Hunter is kissing me, pressing my head against the back of the seat. I feel like I can't breathe. I push him away.

"It's getting late," I whisper. "We should think about heading back."

He gives another big sigh, and looks kind of annoyed. "You know I want more than this, Grace," he says, fiddling with the car keys, trying to start the engine. "It feels like you're always holding something back."

"I don't know what you mean," I protest. But I do, I guess. Hunter wants things to be really serious between us, like we're the only two people in the universe. I'm just not ready for that. I like things the way they are— romantic and fun, a refuge from all the stress of school and home.

"Just don't wait too long," he warns, reversing the car out of its space, turning it away from the tumbling gray sea. "I'm not going to be around much longer."

"I hate it when you threaten me." I fold my arms and look out the window.

"I hate it when you talk like everything else in

194

your life is more important than us," he retorts, and we barely exchange another word all the way home.

Emily seems to have softened a little toward me, especially after I ask her if we can have lunch now and then, whenever she's free. I tell Hunter that I can't have lunch with him every single day of the week, which makes him even more pissed with me than usual. I try to tell him that I'm losing my best friend, but he just rolls his eyes and acts like this is another black mark against me. I never thought it would be so hard to be a good girlfriend.

Emily and I decide to have lunch on Tuesday. I don't say anything to her about the audition at first, because I'm wary of annoying her again. Between bites of cafeteria food, I ask her lots of questions about the school newspaper and which of her photographs are going to be in the next issue. She's pretty bubbly about it.

"I think I've finally found my calling, G," she says, waving a slice of pizza around in the air. "I've been wasting my time with the drama club."

"But you've always loved the drama club!"

"Yeah." She shrugs. "But let's face it—I'm never going to be an actress. It's time for me to get real."

That's what Sonia was talking about—growing up and getting real. Maybe she was right, and I'm just slow to get the point.

"You're not going to quit, are you?" I ask her.

"Maybe," she says. "Dreams don't always work out, you know."

"I guess," I respond, my heart sinking. It feels like everyone's trying to discourage me.

The second time we eat lunch together it's Thursday, less than a week until the audition in the city is scheduled to take place. I've tried talking to my mother again about it, but all she does is lecture me about how sensitive I am, and how young I am, and how I need to build up a thicker skin before I start setting myself up for a life of rejection and failure. What she really means is this: my parents hope I'll get distracted by other things, like college and a "real" career, and forget about becoming an actress. Hopefully, Emily will be more supportive.

"So it doesn't look like I'll be able to go to the audition," I tell her after explaining about the call from Nick Smart—she was pretty impressed with that—and describing how my parents are acting all negative about it.

"You could go without telling them," Emily says. "But if they found out, they'd be really angry with you."

"I know," I sigh. "But you know, they wouldn't find anything out, because I'm not going to get a part. I'd seriously consider going and not telling them if it weren't on a school day."

"But didn't Mrs. Lane say that wasn't a problem?"

"She said it was fine to leave school early. I'd have to go at lunchtime to catch a train. But I don't know how long this whole thing will last. I might have to stand in line for hours, and I might not even get home until the evening. My parents would be really mad at me."

"Hmm, that's a tough situation," says Emily sympathetically. "What day is this audition, anyway?"

"Next Wednesday," I tell her, finishing off my sandwich. She flinches. "What's wrong?" I ask.

"That's my birthday," she says in a quiet voice.

"Of course!" I drop my sandwich back into its plastic carton. "Brilliant timing, right? I can tell my parents we're going out for your birthday straight after school—like to the mall, or to your house before we go to the movies. They wouldn't suspect anything!"

Just as I'm getting really excited, I notice that Emily is shaking her head, looking totally disgusted.

"So first you don't even remember it's my birthday," she says, "and then you're all ecstatic because it means you can sneak off to the city by yourself. I'm glad to be of use to you!"

"It's not that I don't want to spend time with you," I tell her. It seems like all I do nowadays is try to persuade people I want to spend time with them. The whole world thinks I'm selfish, apparently.

"No, it's just that you'd rather pretend to be my

friend than actually be my friend," says Emily. She starts throwing all her trash on her tray, getting ready to leave. "Rather than say, 'Oh, hey, it's your birthday, I guess that means I can't go to this lame-ass audition anyway,' you just think about how I can cover for you. Really, I don't know who you are anymore, G."

Emily stands up and stalks away through the cafeteria. I bury my face in my hands, wishing I could rewind the conversation. Maybe I'm not as klutzy as I used to be, but I'm still a complete pro when it comes to sticking my foot in my mouth.

Chapter Eighteen

It's the day of the audition at the Pavilion Theater, and I'm sitting on a train bound for New York City. Nobody knows I'm here except for Mrs. Lane, and she thinks I'm with my mother.

Maybe I should be the good girl I've always been and stay home because my parents know best. But in this case, I don't think they *do* know best. They still think I'm a little girl who needs protecting from the world. I realize that I'm still naive in lots of ways, but that doesn't mean I should hide out in my room and hope that nothing bad ever happens to me. This audition won't be fun, and it might not even lead to anything. But I need to accomplish this goal and not let fear stand in my way: fear of performing in front of strangers, fear of making a fool of myself in public, and fear of getting into trouble with my parents.

I tried to make things up with Emily, but she's pretty much ignoring me now. If there's something going on for her birthday, she hasn't told me about it. I heard some of the other drama club girls talking about going out somewhere together, but when they noticed me they all stopped talking. So any grand gesture I was considering—like skipping the audition and turning up at Emily's house to grovel my way back into her good graces—would be a total waste of time. When I see Emily in class first period, I wish her a happy birthday. She flashes me a brief smile that looks more like a grimace, but doesn't speak. Somehow I don't think she's going to be issuing me a last-minute invitation.

There was no point in trying to discuss my audition dilemma with Tom and Sonia, either. They're both wrapped up in their own worlds. Sonia is obsessed with becoming the valedictorian, so she does nothing but hole up in her room studying. Tom tries to spend as little time as possible at home, and when he is there, it's all raised voices and slammed doors. I'm just an unwanted distraction. I could be coming down with scarlet fever, or planning to run off and join the circus, and nobody would even notice.

I was planning to say something to Hunter, but he was so down on this audition that it just wasn't worth it. He's got this perfect summer planned, where I give him my undivided attention and we spend every possible minute together until he has to leave for college. He got grumpy—or, even worse, brooding and quiet—whenever I tried to talk about it.

"This is something *for* me, not against you," I tried to explain, but Hunter would just shake his head. The way he sees it, I'm just looking for excuses to spend time away from him. I can't begin to tell him how insane that idea is.

It's weird. I'm trying to be true to myself, but that means lying to everyone and saying I'm going out with Emily after school. Even more weird is this—I'd rather be going out with Emily today than sitting on an almost-empty, early-afternoon train, feeling scared and lonely, heading off by myself to an audition in the city. But she didn't invite me, so I'm seizing the day, living in the moment, just like Miss Sara talked about. This reminds me; I haven't sent Miss Sara a get-well-soon card yet. If I have time, I'll buy her something from one of those ritzy places near the station.

Every time the doors between this train car and the next one swing open, I get all paranoid about some friend of the family walking by and spotting me here. But it's pretty quiet at this time of the day, and the only person walking up and down the aisle is the conductor, checking tickets. As the train gets closer to the city, I pull the directions out of my bag for the twentieth time and check my watch again. I have half an hour to get from Grand Central to the theater, but it shouldn't take me nearly that long. The main thing is not to get lost or run over by a taxi, and to try and seem calm when I arrive. I wish someone was with me—my mother, or Emily, or Hunter—just so I wouldn't feel so alone and vulnerable. But sometimes, I guess, you have to do things on your own, especially when it seems like the whole world is against you.

New York City is loud, incredibly bright, and bursting with people. This may not be rush hour, but nobody told Grand Central Station. Everywhere, people are hurrying to catch trains or lining up to buy tickets. Instantly I'm disoriented—how do I get out of this place? Which way is west?—and I get distracted by the beautiful ceiling soaring high above my head. It's a representation of the sky with all its constellations, and it looks utterly vast and overwhelming. This is a city that turns ordinary people into stars, I tell myself, pausing to gaze in awe for a moment. Then someone rushing past jostles me, and I spin around, clutching my bag. This *isn't* a city where people just stand around staring and dreaming—it's about action. I have to get a move on, find my way down the right corridor, and make my way west to Broadway.

Despite all the chaos of the traffic and crowds, not to mention the neon and billboards of Times Square, I manage to make it to the theater in fifteen minutes.

The Pavilion is one in a line of three on West Forty-fourth Street. I tug on the huge brass handles of the main glass doors and discover that they are locked. Maybe I don't have the right day or time. Maybe too many girls have already turned up and they've simply closed the doors.

Then I remember the stage door. Sure enough, down a stinky alleyway alongside the theater is a black door propped open with a chair. I hesitate for a second and then march down the alley toward it. Just as I'm about to stride in like I own the place, a burly security guard steps out and we collide. Or rather, I collide with his giant belly and ricochet back into the alley.

"Watch yourself," he says. "Auditioning?"

"Yup," I respond with a nod.

"Along the corridor, up the stairs, second on the left."

He stands aside to let me pass. My heart is in my mouth. I hope this is the right stage door, and that I don't find myself auditioning for a strip club or something. Walking along the corridor gives me no clues at all. It's pretty dingy back here, some stacked chairs outside one door, a handwritten sign that says SMOKE OUTSIDE tacked to the peeling wall. If this is a real Broadway theater, it's not very glamorous. I turn to climb the grubby stairs, and that's when the sound of voices hits me—girls' voices. There's a long line of girls wending its way down the stairs. Some are by themselves; most have at least one adult with them. I guess the line isn't moving very quickly, because some are sitting on the stairs, looking bored and tired.

I shuffle into place behind the last girl in line—she's in her late teens, her hair in a ballet bun—and tap her on the shoulder.

"Excuse me, is this the right place for the *Anne of Green Gables* audition?" I whisper. She turns around and looks at me like I've just trekked dog poop across her bedroom carpet.

"I guess," she says, in a voice that suggests it's a stupid question, and turns away again.

The line does move, but only in bursts, and as I get higher up the stairs, I realize that they're letting girls through in groups of six or eight. Forty minutes later I'm nearly at the door that leads to the corridor, and the line behind me stretches right down the stairs. Forty minutes is long enough to feel every possible emotion, from excitement about my first real audition to remorse about lying to my family; from optimism about singing "Since I Don't Have You" to despair at my lack of experience. Because I have nobody to talk to, I'm able to eavesdrop on all the conversations going on around me. Lots of the girls seem to know each other—they call each other's names up and down the stairs—and I can hear conversations about other auditions, about commercials girls are going up for, about summer theater and touring productions and past tours with *The Will Rogers Follies*.

"Do you wanna see my new head shots?" one girl asks another, and I can't help trying to steal a glance myself, even though she's too far away for me to see anything clearly. "They cost a thousand bucks. . . ."

"No!" gasps the other girl.

"But they're totally cool—look."

"Mine only cost six hundred," the other girl says. "But that's because my agency did a deal."

Eek! This is just what I was worried about. These girls range in age from about ten to their mid-twenties, by the looks of it, but they all seem so confident and professional. I'm the only idiot novice here, completely out of my league.

When nearly an hour has passed, the girl in front of me turns to look down her nose at me again.

"Which part?" she says.

"Sorry, what?" I ask, when I click that she's talking to me.

"Which part are you here for?" she says.

"Oh! I'm not sure. I mean, whatever," I burble. I don't even know what parts are on offer, but I don't want to admit it to her. I don't have to worry about more conversation, though, because the girl with the perfect bun gives a tiny snort of derisive laughter and then turns her back on me.

Finally, after more than an hour waiting on the stairs and along the corridor, I end up in a small rehearsal room with mirrors down one wall, a battered piano in the corner, and very dirty windows. The room is full of people, although all parents, guardians, and agents have been asked to stand outside rather than crowd into the room with the rest of us. My eyes swim and my head is thumping. I wait my turn to sign in at a table and get my audition number.

"Sign there and there," a short woman with spiky red hair tells me, without looking up from the stack of papers in front of her. "Take this number and stick it to your top—I don't care how, just stick it. Fill out this form and attach it to your resume and shot."

"I'm sorry . . . I don't have a resume or . . . or anything."

She sniffs, still not looking up. "Then just put your agent's address."

"I . . . I don't have an agent. Sorry." I'm trying to keep my voice down, but it feels like all the girls behind me in line are staring, and probably laughing at my hopeless inadequacy.

"Whatever," sighs the redhead, as though I'm being difficult. "We just need a contact number, okay? Fill it in, step to the side. Let's keep this line moving, ladies."

Really, I might as well leave the sheet blank, but I fill in my home address and number, and add it to the huge pile at the end of the table. While I wait in the corner of the room, I pat my sticky number—it's 309—onto my chest and look at the girls standing at the table. It looks like everyone has a photograph—a "head shot"—and a professional resume in their hands. Who am I trying to kid, turning up here today like I know what I'm doing?

Standing in the cluster of girls waiting by the window, I try to work out exactly what's going on. Nobody's doing anything that even remotely resembles auditioning. It feels like we're cattle in a holding pen.

"I wish they'd hurry up," one girl whispers to me. She has curly hair like Emily, and is dressed head to toe in green. She's the first person who's smiled at me since I got to New York.

"What happens now?" I whisper back.

"Weeding," she mutters.

"What's that?" I know I sound like a fool, but this girl doesn't look like she'll make fun of me for being a newbie.

"Weeding out all the girls who can't sing."

"But surely everyone can sing," I say. "Otherwise they wouldn't be here."

"This is your first audition, right?"

I nod.

"Just wait." She looks at me and grins, then gestures with her head to the man and woman holding a conversation sotto voce in the middle of the room.

"Okay—next group," calls the man, reading from his clipboard. "Numbers 290 through 299. Hurry, hurry. Line up here."

Girls of all shapes and sizes scurry into position, all standing in a line in front of him. The pianist, who looks like he's wearing a pajama jacket, plays the first line of "The Star-Spangled Banner."

"All right, ladies—the national anthem," shouts the man. "All together, on the count of three."

Some of the girls glance at each other nervously, but they all start more or less together, the piano booming out in the corner.

"Oh, say can you see by the dawn's early light," they sing, and the woman paces down the line, pausing behind each girl. It sounds pretty good to me at first, but after a line or two, some of the girls start stumbling over the words, and when they get to the tricky part, where it goes really high, it sounds like only two of the whole line can manage it. They finish singing, and the man and the woman confer.

"Numbers 292 and 295," calls the man. "Please wait in that corner. Everyone else, thanks very much. You're free to leave."

"See?" The girl in green nudges me as the downcast rejects troop past us and out the door.

"I thought we'd get to sing our own audition song," I

whisper to her. I'm utterly terrified now. What if I don't even make it through the anthem? I start feeling panicky.

"They do this when too many people turn up," she tells me. "Sometimes you have to sing the first verse and chorus of 'Tomorrow.' The weak singers always crack right away on that one. Remember to sing loud and stay in key, if you can. I'm Chessy, by the way. Short for Francesca."

I'm about to tell Chessy my name, but the man is shouting for the next group—300 through 309. I'm on! I take my place in the line, staring out at the girls waiting to sign in at the table, most of whom are looking at us with a sort of hostile curiosity.

"Okay, ladies—in order, please." The man organizes us so we're standing in numerical order. Chessy is the first girl in my group; I'm the last. The girl who was in front of me on the stairs stands next to me, her chin high in the air. I stick mine higher, in the hopes it'll bring me confidence. "You know the drill. On the count of four—two, three, four."

I open my mouth and hope for the best. Really. At least I've had a lot of practice at singing the anthem this year, because of all the football games I attended. All the singing rehearsals and voice lessons I did for *Grease* have helped a lot as well, and the high notes don't feel like a problem. I remember Chessy's advice, and sing as loud as I can. I'm in such a blind panic that I can't hear anyone else, and the piano sounds like it's in a distant room. Barely are the words *home of the brave* out of my mouth, and the man with the clipboard is shouting out numbers and telling everyone else they can leave. I'm in such a fog, I don't even know if I'm supposed to stay or go.

"Come on." It's Chessy's voice. "You're through."

"I am?" I follow her to the other side of the room.

"Yeah—you, me, and the girl next to you."

Thank God I made it through the first round. It all seemed to happen in such a whirlwind—already there's another line of agitated girls getting ready to sing.

"Now they'll sort us by whatever they're looking for," Chessy confides, pulling me closer to the mirrored wall.

"What do you mean?" I ask, nervous about this new hurdle that seems to have nothing to do with singing or acting.

"You know, age or size, or maybe hair color," she explains. "If one of the leads is really short, they don't want the girl playing his sister to tower over him. If the leading lady is a blonde, she may not want too many other blondes in the chorus. And they might be looking for someone who looks like she's twelve, say, to fill a particular role."

"Really?" I thought it was all about talent, but I'm beginning to see that it's partly about luck. Maybe my hair is too dark and my legs are too long; maybe they don't need any more sixteen-year-old girls. I've survived the first "weeding" room, but maybe the next person with a clipboard will take one look at me and send me off to catch an early train.

"Listen up," says clipboard man, walking toward our group. "The first group of numbers I call, go to the room at the end of the corridor. Second group, you're in the room two doors away. I'm only going to read these once, so pay attention."

Chessy says good-bye—she's in the first group, and I'm in the second—and I walk to the next room in a total daze. The girl from the stairs is in front of me again, but ignoring me completely. She pushes through the door ahead of me. Our new destination is a room even smaller than the last, empty of any furniture apart from two chairs, both with their backs to the door. One is empty. In the other sits a woman: she's dressed in black, apart from her sneakers, with glasses pushed up on her head, scribbling notes as we walk in.

"Come in, come in," she says, slapping down her pen. "Ladies, when I call your number, step forward and sing me your audition piece, a cappella. The rest of you, keep it down. When you finish, you can leave by the back stairs as quietly as possible. If we want to see you again, we'll call you. Okay?"

Oh my God. This is worse than the other room. I

knew I'd have to sing by myself at some point, but I thought it would be onstage, looking out at the producers sitting amid a sea of red velvet seats, with a pianist accompanying me. Instead, I'm in this stuffy room, singing without any musical help, while a whole lot of unfriendly girls I don't know stand listening and staring at me, all of them hoping that I suck. This shouldn't freak me out, I know. Didn't I just perform onstage in front of hundreds of people? But this is much more intimidating—fluorescent lights, a hostile crowd, nobody pulling for me in the audience or backstage.

The door opens again, and an older man with silver hair and silver-rimmed glasses slips into the room. He drops into the empty chair and whispers something to the woman.

"Right," she says. "Okay, number 283—you're first."

Each girl who takes her turn seems pretty good. Some of them are *really* good. They come across as totally confident and accomplished. My turn creeps closer and closer, and my stomach twists itself into hard knots. My chest is so tight, I don't know how I can keep breathing, let alone sing.

After some girls finish, the man and the woman confer in whispers. Sometimes the woman makes notes, and the man just sits there cleaning his glasses on his shirtsleeve. I wish Chessy were in this room so she could interpret all this for me. I can't work out what's good and what's bad. One by one, girls sing and leave, some waving good-bye to their friends, until there's just me and the mean girl from the stairs left. The man checks his watch and stretches, like he's completely exhausted. The mean girl stands up and sings "We Kiss in a Shadow" from *The King and I*. It's a really beautiful song, and she does a good job of it, smiling all the way through like she's in a beauty pageant. I don't feel capable of smiling, but that's okay—my song is sad.

Finally it's my turn. At first I'm hopeful that it'll just be me and the man and woman in the room when I sing, but as I cross the room to take my spot, the girl who just sang is hanging around, pretending to pack her bag—probably waiting to see the idiot amateur mess up—and then the door opens and a new group of girls troops in. I have to stand there fidgeting, feeling like I'm about to fall over, while the woman makes her speech about everyone keeping quiet.

"When you're ready," she says, giving me a curt nod.

"I don't have plans and schemes," I sing. *"And I don't have hopes and dreams. I don't have anything, since I don't have you."*

Suddenly, Miss Sara's voice is in my head. *Stay in the moment*, she says. *Make everyone in the room feel it.* And maybe it's because I feel completely hopeless about this strange audition, totally anonymous and exposed, but every line of the song seems to ache with sadness and despair.

"Thank you," says the woman when I finish. The silver-haired man looks at me but doesn't speak. "You're free to go."

I make my way out of the theater and back to the station in a foggy daze. I'm in time for the 5:17 train back to Cumberland, but it's crowded and I have to stand all the way home. Perhaps because the train is full of commuters, I feel like I'm returning from a hard day in the city, too.

I don't feel exhilarated or even relieved that the audition is over. I don't know if I did well enough to get a part, or if doing well even mattered if my face doesn't fit. All I know is this: I went to a Broadway audition and sang my heart out. Not getting a part in the show seems more likely than not, and this will be my first failure. But I can handle it—really. I keep telling people that I'm growing up, and today I felt it, perhaps for the first time.

Chapter Nineteen

On the long train ride home, I make some decisions. It's time to face up to things in my life. If I want more independence, then lying to everybody isn't really going to cut it. It makes me feel pretty miserable, and beside that, it makes going for the audition seem like some stupid teen rebellion. I wanted to audition today because I'm determined to gain more experience, and I'm not prepared to give up my dreams of acting on the stage just because it's going to get harder from here on in. Now, even if I don't go to another audition for eons, I'll know what to expect and I can be a little more prepared. This is what I have to make my parents understand. I have to tell them where I went today, even if it means I'm grounded for life.

I let myself into the house just as they're finishing dinner. Rascal bounds up to me, wagging his tail, and I stop to give him a pat, listening to the familiar sounds of chairs scraping back, dishes clattering, and Sonia talking about how much work she has to do. I feel more nervous than I did when I was singing unaccompanied in the horrible room at the theater. So I take a deep breath and call out that I'm home.

"We weren't expecting you yet, honey," says my mother when I walk into the kitchen. Tom isn't home yet, apparently, and Sonia disappears off to her room, claiming she has a test to study for. Dad is rinsing the dishes, and my mother is covering leftovers and trying to fit them into our overcrowded fridge. "Emily said you were all going out to eat and wouldn't be back till late."

"Emily said that?" I ask, suddenly nervous.

"Yes, when I called," says my mother, peering at me around the fridge door. "Didn't she mention it? You were all in the hot tub, I guess—I could hear you all squealing and giggling. I'm surprised you still have a voice left. At least you didn't get your hair wet."

So Emily covered for me—that means she can't be totally annoyed with me! But then I remember what I've decided to do: no more lies. I clear my throat, but somehow I can't get the first words out.

"What's the matter, Gracie?" My father rinses the last plate and stacks it in the dishwasher. "Did you girls have a quarrel?"

"No," I say, shaking my head, trying to pluck up my courage. "It's just . . . Mom, Dad, I've got something to tell you. Would you come and sit down, please?"

My parents go from cheerful to sick with worry in a flash. Part of me wants to make up another lie right away, just to avoid this whole conversation. But I stick to my guns and confess everything. I tell them how I've been in the city this afternoon to attend the audition. Surprise, surprise—they're really mad at me. My mother buries her head in her hands, and my father goes red in the face, his mouth set in a hard line. I have to plead with them to let me finish what I have to say.

"I know that going without your permission was wrong," I say. I'm trying so hard to stay calm, not to burst into tears. "And I understand why you didn't want me to go, and that you're only trying to protect me from disappointment. But you have to know that this was really important to me—not because I think I'm going to get a part in this show. I know I don't have a shot."

"Then why did you lie to us and sneak off?" demands my father.

"I . . . I don't know how to explain this exactly." I falter. "But I needed to put myself through this so I know what's in store for me. You tell me that I don't know how tough things are in the real world—well, I want to see for myself. It's not that I don't believe you, but if I don't experience this for myself, I'll just be living in some fairy tale, dreaming about being a big star. Then

217

I'll be completely unprepared for the reality of it. And you've always brought us up to be . . . what's the word . . . pragmatic?"

My mother nods in spite of herself, and my father frowns at her.

"Gracie, we want you to be prepared for life," he says sternly. "But you've got plenty of time to learn about the real world. You're only sixteen, for God's sake."

"But I'm already expected to learn more about responsibility," I say, keeping my voice low and steady. I don't want this to escalate into a screaming row, as usual. "Like balancing schoolwork and a social life. And preparing for the SAT and college applications in the fall."

"That's different," grumbles my father.

"We have complete confidence that you'll do well in your tests and schoolwork," my mother tells me. "You're an intelligent girl and a hard worker. But the world of professional theater is something else, Grace. It's very, very competitive. Hardly anyone makes it, and you're being judged on all sorts of things beyond your control. Being talented isn't enough. They might be looking for a different type altogether."

"Like someone shorter, or someone with blond hair, right?" I smile to myself, thinking of the conversation with Chessy. "That's one of the things I learned today. See, this is what I'm trying to explain. I know this now—I saw it for myself. I saw the way all the girls were treated like cattle, and the way so many of them were sent home before they even got a chance to sing their audition piece. I saw how we all were divided up by things like height and age. And I saw how talented the girls in my group were. But none of this makes me disillusioned. It just means I've wised up. I know how high the bar is now, and it gives me something to aim toward in the future."

"And it's a bar that keeps moving all the time," says my mother, reaching out a hand to smooth back my hair. "We just don't want you to feel frustrated and inadequate."

"Or rejected," adds my father. He looks less irate now, more sort of pensive and sad.

My mother nods. "Look what it's doing to Tom right now. Look what it's doing to all of us."

"But just because Tom is getting rejection letters from colleges doesn't mean you want him to give up, right?" I gaze over at my father. "You want him to keep trying—that's what you always taught us. Rejection's just part of life, and we have to learn how to deal with it."

"Yes, but—"

"And I know I probably got rejected today," I say, looking him in the eyes. "I was just one of hundreds there, and lots of the girls had much more experience than me. But I'm cool with it, really. I can handle it. You think I'm still too young to deal with this, but I have to start somewhere."

"I know," sighs my mother. "I just wish you hadn't lied to us about it. First the party, now this."

"Lying about going to the party was stupid and selfish—I know that, Ma. But this is different, and that's why I wanted to tell you about it. I could have just pretended to be out with Emily, but I didn't want to keep lying."

"You really went into the city by yourself?" asks my father, and I nod. "Gracie, you're taking years off my life. You could have been mugged, or kidnapped, or . . ."

He breaks off in despair at my rash behavior.

"Were the other girls friendly?" asks my mother. She's mellowed now. Rascal is nudging her knee, and she reaches down to scratch behind his ear.

"This one girl talked to me and explained what was happening," I tell her. "Most of the time I was just standing in line waiting to get my number. And the audition was over pretty quickly."

"Where was this theater, anyway?" asks my father.

"West Forty-fourth Street," I mutter.

"Times Square!" groans my father. "Next time, you go with your mother, all right? No more running around New York City by yourself. I want you to promise, Grace."

"And I want you to eat some dinner," says my mother. "You must be starving."

She's right—giant pangs of hunger have replaced the anxious knots twisting in my stomach. So even though I don't think there's going to be a next time for a long time, I promise my father that I won't go back to the city alone. We all get up from the table and walk into the kitchen, where my mother retrieves the leftovers from the fridge. I sit at the counter while she heats things up in the microwave, swinging my legs and telling my parents all about the audition—the long line, singing the national anthem, not even realizing when my number got called out. I feel so much better now that this is out in the open. So I make another promise—a silent one to myself—to get *everything* out in the open, beginning with telling Hunter about the audition.

After I finish eating, I send Hunter a text message, asking him to call or drop by. Twenty minutes later the doorbell rings.

"I'll get it," I call, hurrying down the stairs. Hunter's standing on the doorstep scratching his head, looking drop-dead gorgeous in his T-shirt and jeans. My heart sinks at the thought of telling him that I've been less than honest.

"I came as soon as I got your message," he says, his handsome face all concerned. "I thought you were out with Emily tonight."

I step out onto the porch, closing the door behind me, and walk over to the creaky swing. Hunter follows me, dropping onto the seat next to me. When I shiver—more from nerves than from the cold—he throws a protective arm around my shoulders.

"That's what I wanted to talk to you about," I tell him. "I didn't go to Emily's birthday thing. Actually, I wasn't invited."

Hunter looks puzzled. "Why didn't you tell me? We could have gone out somewhere. Forget Emily—"

"No," I interrupt, gently placing a hand on his knee. "It's . . . well, I went somewhere else today. I caught a train into the city and went to the audition. I know I shouldn't have lied about it—that's why I wanted to tell you now. I just told my parents."

"I can't believe you, Grace," he says, his face hard, his body tense and rigid. "What do you think you're doing?"

"I just . . . I guess I just really wanted to go to the audition—"

"I don't mean about the audition! I mean with you and me. Why the hell are you lying to me?"

"I didn't mean—"

"Look, are you my girlfriend or not?" Now he's raising his voice. I thought he'd be annoyed with me, but not this angry.

"Of course I'm your girlfriend!"

"Then why are you trying to make a fool of me?"

"I'm not!" I protest, completely flustered. "What are you talking about?"

"You're treating me like I'm an idiot. You're acting as though *we* don't matter at all. You're just gonna do what you want, whenever you want, and if I don't like it, too bad."

He stands up like he's going to leave, and I reach out to grab his arm.

"Hunter—please, just listen to me." We're both distracted for a moment as the Wagon pulls into our driveway, blinding us with its headlights. It's Tom, getting out of the car and walking along the path toward us. I lower my voice and appeal to Hunter. "Please, just sit down. Let's talk about this."

"No," he says, tugging his arm free in so violent a movement, I fall forward, almost spilling off the swing seat.

"Hey!" shouts Tom, bounding up the steps. "What do you think you're doing, Wells?"

"Get out of my face," says Hunter, his voice thick with contempt. "This is none of your business."

"I think your pushing my little sister around *is* my business," says Tom angrily. He shoves Hunter so hard that Hunter staggers back toward me. "Not so big and tough now, are you?"

"Tom!" I plead, clinging to Hunter so he won't retaliate. "Just leave us, please!"

"You should have dumped him months ago like I told you," Tom says, staring Hunter down. "You're too good for a dumb jock like him."

Hunter strides toward Tom and pushes him, but Tom's ready for him. They grab each other's shoulders and start grappling.

"What do *you* know, loser?" Hunter spits, sending Tom crashing onto the floorboards.

"Stop it—both of you!" I shout, leaping to my feet. With all this noise, any second now my parents are going to come out, and we'll all be in the worst trouble. But they're not listening to me. Tom grabs Hunter by the ankles and drags him down to the ground, where they wrestle and roll around. One minute Tom's on top, trying to throttle Hunter; the next Hunter has rolled him over and is throwing wild punches.

"Please stop!" I try to pull Hunter off, but all this does is give Tom the break he needs to push Hunter onto his back.

"Keep away from my sister," Tom hisses, pummeling Hunter like a crazy man. "She doesn't want anything to do with you."

"Shut your stupid mouth!" Hunter kicks Tom off and scrambles to his feet. "I know what Grace wants, not you!"

That's it. I've totally had it with these two morons.

"STOP—THIS—NOW!" I shriek, kicking at them

both. They're both so out of breath, and surprised that I'm joining the fight, they stop attacking each other and look at me, almost as though they forgot I was there. "Just cut it out, okay? You're both totally stupid and ridiculous. Tom, I don't need you to come to my rescue like I'm some little girl. And, Hunter, I'm not some piece of property you have to defend. Just grow up, both of you. I'm so sick of you pretending this is about me and saying how *you* know what I want, when all you care about is your own stupid male egos. If either of you really cared about me, you would LISTEN to me once in a while instead of always thinking you know best."

I stand there with my hands on my hips, and nobody says anything. Then the front door bursts open, and my father steps out, scowling.

"What's with all the noise out here?" He sees Tom and Hunter slumped on the ground—Tom with a bloodied nose, one hand gripping Hunter's torn T-shirt, and Hunter with red marks flaming on his bare neck. His expression changes from annoyed to enraged. "What the . . . ? Grace, get inside."

I don't argue. I don't try and stand up for Tom or Hunter, or explain what was going on. When I said I'd had it with both of them, I was telling the truth. I step over Hunter's legs and walk into the house. My father slams the door shut, and I can hear his raised voice, giving both of them a piece of his mind.

"Gracie, what's happening out there?" calls my mother from the living room. I walk over to her, shaking my head. "It sounded like World War Three."

"It's just Tom and Hunter," I say, plopping down on the ground by her feet. I gaze up at her. "Ma, why are boys so stupid?"

She smiles, rubbing the top of my head. "It's not easy being eighteen, I suppose," she says.

"It's not easy being sixteen." I give a deep sigh. "When do things start getting easier?"

"Oh, Grace," says my mother, sounding wistful all of a sudden. "I hate to tell you this—but I don't know if they ever do."

Chapter Twenty

The atmosphere in the car going to school the next morning is pretty tense, to say the least. Maybe my parents have clued Sonia in about last night's porch brawl. She doesn't say a word either to me or Tom the whole way there, though she must have noticed that Tom's nose is still kind of messed up, and there's a red scratch above his left eye. Tom doesn't complain when I call shotgun, and I try to avoid looking at him as I get in and out of the car. I'm so mad at him for starting that fight with Hunter, and I'm mad at Hunter, too, for reacting in such a hotheaded way, even when I begged him to stop. My mother gave me a big talk last night about boys that age not knowing how to handle their strong emotions and finding it hard to express their feelings and frustrations. Whatever. I just want to get away from their feelings and frustrations for a while, and have some quality time with a girlfriend.

At school, Emily is acting pretty cool toward me

again. But I grab her before classes start and pull her aside, thanking her for covering for me, and telling her that I confessed everything to my parents anyway.

"That's good," she says. "Glad it all worked out."

"Em, I wanted to remind you about something," I tell her, ignoring the I'm-bored-and-annoyed look on her face. "A week from Saturday—remember what day it is?"

Emily shrugs.

"The Diamond Nights Dance," I say.

Emily rolls her eyes. "What, you want me to help you get ready?" she demands.

"No, silly. Why would I be going to the Diamond Nights Dance?" Emily and I have boycotted it like, forever.

"I don't know—because you and Hunter are trying to get elected king and queen or something? Isn't that what all the Blue Lobsters and their girlfriends want, deep down?"

"I don't care about the Blue Lobsters," I tell her. "I'm all Blue Lobstered out right now. And anyway, I was hoping that you and I could do the usual. The whole Diamond Day thing."

Every year, Emily and I devote that Saturday to certain ritual activities. First, we trawl the mall for some faux diamond accessories—like a tacky belt, or over-the-top costume jewelry—and then we have lunch at

Harris's Hot Dog Stand, as a sort of paean to ballpark food. We each get one of those pedicures where tiny diamante studs are stuck onto your big toenail as extra decoration while the polish is still wet. Then we go back to her house or mine, put on all our accessories—even though we're just wearing jeans and T-shirts—and settle in for an orgy of movie-watching. We always start off with *Gentlemen Prefer Blondes*, because it features the song "Diamonds Are a Girl's Best Friend," and then move on to the great old James Bond film, *Diamonds Are Forever*, finishing up with—what else?—*Breakfast at Tiffany's*, which both of us can practically recite in our sleep. At the stroke of 7 P.M., no matter where we're at with the movies, we stop the DVD and sing "Take Me Out to the Ball Game." I know the whole thing must sound really stupid, but it's more fun than the Diamond Nights Dance any day, not to mention a whole lot cheaper, and with less social anxiety.

Emily's giving me a hard look.

"I thought you'd forgotten," she says quietly. The bell rings, and we head toward first period. "What about Hunter?"

"I don't think he'd look too good in a tiara," I tell her. Now's not the time to fill her in on the whole brother/boyfriend brawl last night. "And the pedicure's on me this year. To make up for missing your birthday yesterday."

"And the hot dogs?" Emily asks as we pass under one of Ms. Schaeffer's elaborate banners for the Diamond Nights Dance. Someone has defaced all the diamonds by drawing on little arms and legs.

"Okay," I say, smiling. "But you have to provide the peanuts."

"Dude, I've still got the ones we didn't eat last year," she says. "They're gross, remember? It's like eating the bodies of dead insects."

"Audrey would never eat them," I agree.

"Audrey wouldn't sing 'Take Me Out to the Ball Game,' either," sighs Emily. "But they probably didn't have baseball in Belgium. Hey, we could have Belgian waffles for dinner. They've got a diamond pattern, right?"

"You're a genius," I tell her, and we smile at each other for what seems like the first time in weeks.

I see Hunter a few times in passing at school. He looks sheepish, as well he might. When I'm stowing books in my locker at the end of the day, he sidles up and puts on his most cute, little-boy face, trying to get the sympathy vote. I try my hardest to stay strong, but it's not easy.

"I know you're mad," he says. "And I know what I did last night was pretty stupid."

"What you *said* wasn't too smart, either," I tell him.

He winces, either because of my barbed comment, or because he's got plenty of Tom-inflicted bumps and bruises.

"I know," he says, hanging his head. "But we do need to talk, you and me. You can't just ignore me forever."

I sigh, shutting my locker door.

"I was thinking," he says quickly, "that maybe we could take a drive out to Mystic this weekend. Just take a walk and, you know, spend some time together. Talk about stuff."

"Talk, or argue?" I ask him. Part of me wants to kiss him and hold him close, but another part of me still has some sense left. I'm just worn out with confrontations, with always having to explain and apologize about everything.

"Just talk. I promise," he says. "Scout's honor."

He gives some weird two-fingered salute.

"I didn't know you were ever a scout," I tell him.

"I wasn't," Hunter admits, hanging his head. He looks up at me, his eyes so intense and blue. "Is it too late to join?"

"Maybe," I say, trying to smile at him, but I'm so tired my face feels immovable. "Listen, I've got drama club—I have to go."

"I'll hang around and give you a ride home, if you want." He perks up, but I shake my head.

"My dad's coming to get me," I say. "And I don't

think that you guys would want to spend much time together right now, huh?"

"I'll see you on Saturday," he says, giving me a rueful smile, and we walk away in different directions.

When my father and I arrive home, I climb up the stairs, dragging my feet. It's still a while until dinner, and even though I don't want to, I know I should try talking to my brother. We live in the same house; we can't avoid each other. I throw my bag into my room and then tap softly on Tom's door.

"Yeah," he says, and I open it a fraction. Tom's sprawled on the bed, throwing a ball into the hoop above his door. It bounces off my forehead when I peek in.

"Ouch!" I rub my head. "Can I come in for a sec?"

"Sure," he says, kind of cold and formal, struggling to sit up.

"I just thought we should talk," I say, closing the door behind me and leaning back against it. Tom says nothing, and I feel my courage ebbing away. It's like we've both said too much already, and now there's just awkwardness and bad feelings. Tom looks at the wall, and out the window, and then finally he speaks.

"I'm sorry about . . . what happened last night. I just thought that he was being a jerk to you, and I wanted to jump in and protect you."

"I don't need protecting," I tell him. "I know you

were trying to help, but I'm a big girl now, and I have to fight my own battles."

"Yeah, I know." Tom sighs and leans back against the headrest.

"It's not just that, anyway—is it?" I ask him.

"What d'you mean?"

"It's not just about defending my honor. You've always had a thing against Hunter."

"I don't have a *thing* against anyone," Tom argues. "But I guess—well, he's not good enough for you, Gracie."

"Shouldn't I be the judge of that?"

"But guys like Hunter Wells—"

"What do you mean, guys *like* Hunter?" I interrupt.

"You know," says Tom, clutching his pillow to his chest. "Guys who think they're hot stuff. Guys who have everything easy in life. They just expect to have things handed to them—girls and good grades and jobs. Places in college."

"Is that what this is all about?" I ask, my voice soft.

"I don't know," Tom says, shaking his head. "Guys like Hunter, they don't have to worry about stuff like college applications. They've got scouts lined up at every game, waiting to snap them up. The rest of us are left fighting over the crumbs. He's the golden boy who can't put a foot wrong—the whole package. Everyone falls for it—teachers, kids at school, college admissions.

I guess I never thought *you'd* fall for it, though."

"I haven't fallen for anything," I tell him, sitting down on the edge of his bed. "Superficially, Hunter may seem like he has it all, but that's not the whole story. His dad left years ago, and his mom's really had to struggle to bring up Hunter and his brothers. He works every summer, just like you, and if he hadn't gotten a football scholarship, he probably wouldn't be going to college at all."

"But he *did* get the scholarship," says Tom bitterly.

"Sure, but it was something he worked hard for, and he's going to have to work even harder to keep it. You know that. And anyway, you can't be angry with him for being an athlete. You're an athlete, too."

"Grace, I run track and play hockey," says Tom drily. "And I'm not real good at either. Nobody's going to hand me tens of thousands of dollars and offer me the college of my choice."

"You can't just dislike Hunter because he plays football—that's nuts. And you can't go around trying to beat people up because you're jealous of what you think they have. You have no idea how much luckier you are!"

"Oh, yeah—how, exactly?"

"You have *us*, you idiot. Parents who've scrimped and saved so you *can* go to college and don't have to worry about getting big scholarships. Sisters who think you're cool and funny and great to hang around with. Even the dog prefers you to anyone else."

"It's only because I feed him stuff at the table," mutters Tom.

"Whatever! My point is, you got some college rejections, and that totally sucks, but you just have to deal with it."

"Really?" he says. "And how would you suggest I do that, Miss Know-it-all?"

"Well, Mr. Sarcastic," I say, "I think you should stop starting fights and trying to interfere in my life. And you should stop moping around your room and snapping everyone's head off if they mention college applications. You can't let a few crummy rejections stand in your way. You have to keep trying."

"And what if I don't want to go to college?"

"I don't believe you," I tell him. "That's just the easy way out. If you're going to start applying to other places, you've got to swallow your pride and stop blaming everyone. It's not Hunter's fault that you didn't get into your college of choice."

"I never said it was," he mumbles.

"And it doesn't matter if you don't like him," I continue. "Unless you know for a fact that he's an ax murderer, I don't want to hear your opinions about him."

"But I don't like the way he treats you—"

"Tom! This is my deal, okay? This is something I

have to sort out myself. It's not like I've fallen over in the yard and scraped my knee and you're going to put a Band-Aid on it and make everything all right. Hunter and I have got some stuff to work out, and we need to do that alone, without members of my family who think they know what's good for me getting in the way."

I hear Mom calling our names, telling us to come downstairs for dinner.

"Everyone's happy to interfere with my life," Tom says, frowning at me. "Nobody ever gets tired of telling me what to do. All Mom and Dad ever talk about is how I'm the black sheep of the family, letting everyone else down."

"It might seem that way, but they're just worried about you," I tell him. "They see how unhappy you are. We all do."

My eyes fill with tears, and I swipe at them with the back of my hand.

"Oh, jeez—don't start crying like a girl," he says gruffly, hitting me with his pillow. "Dad'll kick me down the stairs if he thinks I'm upsetting you again."

"I'm not upset," I insist. "Come on, let's go downstairs. I hate it when we're mad at each other."

Tom swings his legs off the bed and stands up. "You lead the way," he says, and I grin at him, getting to my feet.

"Come on," I say, opening the door.

"Hey, Grace?"

"What?" I look back over my shoulder at him.

"Just one thing before we go downstairs."

"Yeah?"

Tom lowers his voice and looks all conspiratorial.

"I really whipped Hunter, didn't I?" he whispers. "Whipped him *real* good."

I roll my eyes.

"Just shut up," I tell him, and leave the room shaking my head.

Chapter Twenty-one

We drive out to Mystic on Saturday evening. The sky is streaked with gold and orange and red, and out the car window I see birds swooping into the reeds, or flying in graceful formation toward the coast. Dusk is my favorite time of day. It's romantic, I guess, when the light starts to fade and all the colors of the sunset bleed away into a deep blue night sky, sprinkled with brilliant stars.

Hunter parks the car near the harbor, and we retrace our footsteps from our first visit here, walking onto the little bridge and pausing to look out over the water.

"Remember when I kissed you here?" he asks, cuddling me close.

"Of course," I tell him. Like I could ever forget that first kiss! It was one of the most wonderful moments of my life, a feeling I'd dreamed about forever.

"It seems like such a long time ago," he says.

"It was only last fall," I remind him. "Not that

long, really. So much has happened, I guess."

"And this fall I'll be a long way away," he says, and then we both fall silent. Neither of us want to think about it, really—Hunter leaving the state, going off to college. He'll be meeting new people and having a really different sort of life. I'll still be here, stuck in Cumberland, but my life will be different, too. I'll be a senior, getting ready to graduate, applying to colleges, maybe getting the lead in the show again—who knows? I feel a weird mixture of sadness about things changing and excitement about the future.

"Aren't you going to say you'll miss me?" he asks, sounding indignant.

"Of course!" I say, twisting my head so I can see him. He's smiling—only teasing. "You know I will."

"We've had a lot of good times," he says, gazing out over the silvery water.

"A lot of arguments as well," I say ruefully.

"We're kind of tempestuous," he admits, giving me a squeeze. "Especially you."

"We both *want* things," I tell him. "We're not content just to stay in one place."

"Cumberland, you mean?"

"More than that—we both want to go places, do things. Be somebody."

He wraps his arms around me even tighter. "I worry sometimes that you want to push me away."

"No—it's not that." I don't know how to answer this. I want to tell Hunter that part of me wants things to stay the same, for us to be together just as we are tonight, but also that I know that wouldn't be a good thing for either of us. Soon we'll be moving in different directions. Maybe we already are. I wish I knew the right words to say.

Hunter pulls away from me, and suddenly the evening breeze feels cold. He holds out his hand, gesturing toward the other side of the bridge.

"Come on, let's walk," he says, and we stroll across the water into town. For a long time we just walk, hand in hand, past the little shops and restaurants, down narrow streets lined with a cute jumble of houses, meandering back down to the water now and then. Eventually, as the colors of the sky intensify, we find a park bench overlooking the harbor and sit down close to each other. I rest my head on Hunter's shoulder.

"I thought that if we came here, it would be just like last time," he says. There's a sadness in his voice. "But it's different. I guess we didn't really know each other then. Anything was possible."

"What do you mean?" I ask him. "Things are still possible, aren't they?"

"I mean that we know each other now, and we can't idealize each other. You're not the dream girl who I saw dancing around a car in the school parking lot. You're a real person with your own stuff going on. Sometimes I wish you didn't have anything going on except me."

"But you were proud of me, weren't you, when I got the part in the school show?"

"Yeah, you know I was. But ultimately, I guess I'd rather you were always there for me. That's why I get so crazy and jealous—I can't help wanting you all to myself."

"That's not fair," I tell him softly. "You have other things going on, too. You're a Blue Lobster."

"Not for much longer," he points out; then I can feel him shaking with quiet laughter. "Blue Lobster, it sounds so ridiculous!"

"Do you wish I was more like those other girls?" I ask him. "The Blue Lobster girls who know everything about every game, and wait around outside the locker room, and hang around at practice?"

"Maybe," he admits, changing position so I have to lift my head. "Maybe I want you to prove to me that you care about me."

"I can't just drop my friends and drop my life, any more than you can," I tell him.

"Sometimes I think . . . well, that you don't really want me."

"You know I do!" I protest. My mind's in turmoil now, and at first all I can think about is how wrong Hunter is—how he's the prefect boyfriend in so many ways, caring and protective and strong. But then I think of all the times he gets mad at me, how I never seem to live up to his expectations. I always feel like I'm letting him down somehow.

"But I don't think you want to get serious the way I do," he tells me. "I want us to be everything to each other. We don't need other people if we have each other—that's what I figure. It's just you and me. Nobody else matters, and nothing else counts. Otherwise it's just kid's stuff."

Every single part of me aches to tell him that I feel the same way, that I want us to be everything to each other, and to hell with the rest of the world. Aren't I the girl who keeps telling everyone how grown-up I am, how I deserve more independence, more autonomy, more respect? But a little voice inside my head is telling me to slow down. Hunter is my first boyfriend, and maybe he's going to turn into the great love of my life, my one big romance, the soul mate everyone talks about finding. But I'm not ready for that yet. I can't be the kind of girlfriend he wants, no matter how hard I try. I need more time to be myself—to find out who I am and what I want to be.

"Grace," he says, and I turn my face up to his and look deep into his eyes. Even in the fading light they're a startling deep blue, like the sky on a perfect day. "I think . . . I think maybe I'm trying to force something, when if it was meant to happen, it would. Maybe now's not the right time for us. Maybe we met too soon."

"But I can't imagine things without you," I say unhappily.

"I know what you're saying," he says, squeezing my shoulders. "I'm still here. But only for a couple more months."

"It's just . . . I've never felt this way before," I tell him, and he smiles and holds me close.

"I've never felt this way about anyone either," he says, his voice soft as the lapping waves. "I love you."

"I love you, too," I whisper. Looking at Hunter, a strange sadness fills me. I never thought it would be possible to be in love with a boy, but know, in your heart of hearts, that being together isn't the right thing for either of you. And I can see in Hunter's face that he's thinking the same thing.

"This is so hard," he murmurs, pressing a kiss into the side of my head, his lips warm against my hair.

We're both quiet again, watching the seagulls landing on the posts and piers where the fishing boats are moored. The white of their feathers looks so sharp against the dark water slapping against the sides of boats. The colors of the sky seem to be melting away now, and I wish the sunset could stay there, vivid and dreamy and beautiful, just for a little while longer.

* * *

When Hunter drops me off at home and kisses me good night, it's the softest and sweetest of kisses. At last we draw away from each other, but I don't want to get out right away. We linger in the car, heads bent together, our foreheads touching. I close my eyes and feel a strange sense of peace and sadness at the same time. We haven't broken up, but it's hard not to feel this is the end of something.

Inside, my parents are both still up. They're sitting in the living room, but the TV is off, and they stop talking as soon as I walk in, yawning. It takes me a minute to register the looks on their faces—so serious and intense that I worry I've missed my curfew or something.

"Grace," says my mother. "Come and sit down, honey."

"What is it?" I scoot onto the sofa, still thinking about my good-night to Hunter.

"We got a call tonight from the director of your summer camp," says my father, getting to his feet and starting to pace up and down in front of the fireplace. "She said . . . well, Cara, you should tell her."

"Grace," my mother says, and there's a long pause before she speaks again. "I'm afraid it's bad news. I don't know how to tell you this, because I know how much she meant to you, but . . ."

"But what?" I ask, my mind racing.

My mother looks at my father, and then sighs. "I'm so sorry, honey, but Miss Sara has died."

The next morning I wake up hoping it was all a bad dream, but then I remember my mother's long explanation about how Miss Sara never really recovered from her heart attack earlier in the spring. I can't believe it—I don't want to believe it. Miss Sara was the most vibrant, vivacious, *alive* person I've ever known. Everything about her was alive: the bright colors she wore; her loud voice; her even louder laugh; her wide, sparkling smile. Her singing voice rang through a room, and she always walked around camp with her head held high, as though she were on a stage and the world was her audience. I don't know if she even read my e-mail about getting the lead in the school musical—maybe she was already too sick by then to be interested in such nonsense. Without her training, her encouragement, and her words of wisdom, I couldn't have done it. I wish I'd had the chance to tell her that.

I walk around the house in my pajamas, feeling completely miserable. If only I'd sent her a card, or tried to visit her in the hospital! Instead I was so wrapped up in myself, in my own life and minidramas. And now she's gone, and I won't ever be able to thank her. From now on, I swear, I'm going to be a different person. I'm going to think of others and *their* feelings for a change.

At school, Emily is really sympathetic about Miss Sara, asking me to tell her more stories from camp, even though I start crying half the time.

"You shouldn't block it all out," she tells me at lunch as I sit rubbing my red eyes in a corner of the cafeteria. "You have so many positive memories from then, you need to remember every single thing Miss Sara told you."

Hunter is sweet about it, too, leaving his table of Blue Lobsters and coming over to join us.

"It really sucks," he says, gripping my hand. "But Emily's right, you shouldn't bottle stuff up."

"I feel like screaming," I tell them.

"Then why don't we all go sit outside?" Hunter suggests. "Ms. Schaeffer is drilling the cheerleaders out there. Nobody'll hear you over the noise they're making."

I can't help smiling at this, but I don't know when I'll feel like laughing and joking again. All I can think about right now is the fact that Miss Sara is gone forever, and that I was too lazy and self-centered to make the effort to see her one last time.

The week drags on endlessly, and the only thing I'm looking forward to now is my Diamond Day with Emily. She says it'll cheer me up, and I know she's right.

"And you can have the most humongous cry at the end of *Breakfast at Tiffany's*. Really get it all out," she suggests, and I want to hug her for being such a good friend. I've been so crummy to her this semester, really taking her friendship for granted. This stupid ritual of ours actually means something this year. Even Hunter admits it's what I need right now—just a day of hanging out with Emily, doing girlie things and watching old movies, talking and laughing and eating and relaxing. My mother says we can take over our living room for the whole afternoon and evening. She and Dad are going to a golf club dance, and she's told Sonia and Tom that the room is reserved for Diamond Dayers only. They were really cool about it. Tom even offered to steal one of the banners from school as a decoration, but I told him that wouldn't be necessary.

On Thursday evening, I'm setting the table for dinner, digging in the cupboard for the place mats, when the telephone rings.

"Grace, could you get that?" calls my mother. She's making gravy in the kitchen, bent over the stove with her face full of steam. I accidentally pull the whole stack of place mats out of the cupboard and have to jump over them to get to the phone.

"Hello?" I say, wincing at the mess I've made on the floor.

"Grace Giovanni, please."

"This is Grace." I frown because whoever it is has my name wrong.

"Kathy Marx here from Jonathan Carson's office."

This means absolutely nothing to me, so I say nothing.

"From the Carson and Tailor production office," says the woman, sighing as though she realizes she's addressing a ding-a-ling. "Mr. Carson would like you to come in for a second audition."

"What?" I say stupidly.

"This is your callback," she says in a brusque voice. "For *Anne of Green Gables*. He'd like to see you again this Saturday at two, at the Pavilion Theater."

"That's . . . Wow! I mean, that's great." My head is spinning. I can't believe this! The producer wants to see me again—me, Grace di Giovanni! I'm going to have a second audition for an actual Broadway show!

"So we'll see you on Saturday," says Kathy Marx, clearly not amused by my effusion. "Two o'clock at the stage door. Bring your music and make sure you're on time."

I hang up the phone, still in a daze. This is so incredibly exciting! I really didn't think I would make it through to the next round. I'm a nobody from nowhere. All those girls there, with agents, and experience, and fantastic voices . . . and I'm the one getting the callback. This has been the strangest week of my life—so many extreme highs and lows.

"Who was it, honey?" calls my mother, and I walk into the kitchen.

"Someone from . . . someone from the producer's office," I say, stumbling over my words. "The people who are doing the *Anne of Green Gables* musical."

"Really? What did they want?"

"It was a callback. They want to see me for a second audition."

"You're kidding!" My mother turns to look at me, a dripping wooden spoon in her hand. "They want you to audition again?"

And suddenly it hits me: I can't go to this audition. Not only did I promise my parents that the first audition was a one-off just for experience, and that I would focus on my schoolwork for the rest of the school year, Saturday is my big day out with Emily. I can't just drop her because something better has come up. There's no point in having all these good resolutions about being a better person if I immediately start backtracking. She'd be really hurt and angry if I suddenly started acting like a prima donna again, announcing that Diamond Day is off. Our friendship might never recover.

"Yeah," I tell my mother. "But I don't want to go."

"You don't?" My mother looks skeptical. "When is it?"

"Saturday," I say, avoiding her eyes. "But I really don't want to go."

I turn on my heel to leave.

"Grace!" my mother says. "Are you sure about this?"

"Absolutely sure," I say, but my voice wavers, and I know my mom doesn't believe me. Before she can say anything else, I hurry out, back to the phone. I need to dial *69 right away and get Kathy Marx's number so I can call to cancel—before I change my mind.

Chapter Twenty-two

Saturday morning dawns bright and sunny—the kind of day that makes you feel like summer's just around the corner. My mood doesn't really match it, unfortunately. Between my big talk with Hunter, the news about Miss Sara, and then calling the producer's office to turn down the second audition, I feel like this past week has been pretty rocky. I know I'm doing the right thing by sticking to my plans with Emily, but a huge part of me is screaming, *Cancel everything and get yourself to the audition!* My parents were right: if I'm serious about pursuing this as a career, I'll have lots of other chances to audition for shows. I should just be flattered to get the callback and leave it at that.

Emily's scheduled to arrive here around ten, so I drag my butt out of bed and into the shower. I have to get myself together before we head off to the mall. If I spend the whole day moping and fretting, it'll ruin everything. I have to be in the moment, just like Miss Sara said.

Downstairs, my mother is in a strange mood. She keeps forgetting where she put things and getting all flustered. She's always like this before a dance at the golf club; it's the adult version of Diamond Nights, I guess, where everyone's totally judging you by what you wear and how your hair is done. She has an appointment at what passes for a ritzy salon in Cumberland early this afternoon for the full works: hair, nails, and makeup.

In fact, everyone's up and about this morning, making a lot of noise. The usual weekend car negotiations are going on. Dad has to drop me and Emily off at the mall, because Sonia has first dibs on the Wagon today— she and some of her boring friends are driving to Yale for some end-of-year debate team yawnfest. Tom is pretending he wants the car as well, mainly to annoy Sonia, because the rest of us know that one of his friends is driving him up to Hartford today, to look around a college campus. He's just started a second round of applications, much to the relief of my parents—to all of us, really.

"Grace, I've made you some eggs," says my mother, sliding a plate in front of me.

"Ma! You know I'll be eating lunch in, like, two hours. I wasn't going to eat breakfast."

"Who are you—Paris Hilton?" says my father from behind his newspaper. "We're not wasting food in this house."

"Just eat up, please." My mother hands me another plate, this one piled with toasted English muffins. "I don't want you filling yourself up with junk. Now, where did I put the coffeepot?"

"In the sideboard," Tom tells her, his mouth full of cereal. "Cupboard on the left. On top of the china, I think."

"Why didn't you tell me before?" My mother looks horrified.

"I thought that's where you wanted it," he says, letting milk dribble from his mouth and trying to catch my eye. I make a face to show how gross he is. "You know I never question your maternal authority."

"Tom, get the coffeepot for your mother," my father orders, still obscured behind the paper.

"I don't know what's wrong with me today," says my mother. Tom opens the cupboard door and hands her the coffeepot. "What time is it again?"

"Ma, you've asked us that twice in the last ten minutes," I tell her. "It's just after nine thirty."

"Well, as soon as you've finished your breakfast, go upstairs and brush your teeth. When Emily gets here, your father needs to take you to the mall. He has to get back here right away for . . . for . . ."

"For other duties," sighs my father, shaking the newspaper.

"Okay, Okay," I say, scooping up another forkful of eggs. My mother is crazy today, really. If I'd known she was going to be so nuts, we could have asked Emily's parents to drive us to the mall. So much for having a share of the Wagon. I think Rascal has a better chance of borrowing it than I do.

Because my mother's so antsy, I'm all ready—teeth brushed, lips glossed, shoelaces tied—and waiting downstairs when Emily arrives. Emily bounces in, looking so excited about our day that I know I've made the right decision. I didn't even tell her about the call for the audition. Why spoil things?

"You look pretty," I tell her. She's given up on the Sandy-style bob, and her hair is its usual mass of exuberant curls.

"I got the jacket for my birthday," she says, spinning around so I can admire it. It's beige suede, really soft to touch. "Hey, why don't you ask Sonia if you can borrow her leather jacket?"

"Dude, she won't even let me look at it," I whisper, because Sonia is clomping down the stairs right toward it.

"You want to borrow my jacket?" she says. Sonia must have supernatural powers of hearing. "Here you go."

She throws it to me. I'm so startled by her relaxed attitude and uncharacteristic generosity, I nearly drop it.

"What will you wear?" I ask her, still amazed that she's handing over her prize possession.

"Oh, don't worry about me," she says breezily. *"Pas de problem."*

This day just gets stranger and stranger. First my mother is racing around like the Energizer Bunny, and now Sonia is acting all laid back.

"Grace!" My mother pounces just as I'm pulling on Sonia's jacket. It's my favorite of all her clothes— tailored black leather with really narrow lapels. I can't believe I'm actually getting to wear it. "If you two are ready to go . . ."

"Dad!" I call. "We're ready!"

My father appears holding the folded newspaper in his hands, apparently in no hurry at all. He hasn't even got his shoes on. He just stands there, looking at me like I'm speaking in a foreign tongue.

"Actually, Grace," says my mother, turning red as a beet. "Actually, your dad's not taking you."

"What? But I thought . . . how are we going to get there?"

"Look outside," says Emily, her face splitting with a huge smile. She pulls open the front door and I peer out. Parked right outside is a black Honda—Hunter's car! And there's Hunter sitting in the driver's seat, waving to me.

I spin around and look at Emily. "What's going on?" I ask. "You got Hunter to drive us to the mall?"

"Oh, we're not going to the mall," she says. She's so excited, she's almost bouncing. "Hunter's driving us to the station."

I still don't get it. I look over at my mother, who seems to be about ready to burst into tears, and to my father, who's still saying nothing.

"Dude!" says Emily, grabbing my arm. "We're going to the audition! You and me!"

"But . . . but how do you . . . and how can we . . . ?" I drop my hands, completely helpless, and gaze at my mother.

"Don't be angry with me, Grace," she says. "But I called back the production office and told them you could make the audition after all. Don't worry, I cleared it with Emily first."

"How did you get the number?" I really can't take all of this in.

"With some difficulty," my mother admits. "I had to call Mrs. Lane on Friday, and she contacted Nick Smart, and between us we pieced it all together."

"So . . . so, you're okay with this?" I'm kind of addressing everyone now—my mother, my father, Emily.

"You started this crazy business of auditioning for a Broadway show," says my father with a shrug. "You might as well finish it."

"Here," says my mother, handing me something: it's the sheet music for "Since I Don't Have You." "The lady at the producer's office said you'd need to bring this with you."

"Thanks," I say, my brain still in a fog. "And Hunter . . . he didn't know . . . did you call him?"

"I did," Emily says. "That dude is way proud of you. He offered to drive us to New London so we can catch the express. Which means we have to leave, like, this minute. As your official chaperone, I can't allow you to be late for your audition. We have to catch the ten forty-seven to make it into the city on time."

"She's right, off you go!" says my father, stepping forward to hug me good-bye.

Then my mother embraces me, holding me tight. "Miss Sara would be so proud of you," she whispers. "Just go and do your best."

"I will, Ma," I promise. "Thank you so much."

"Come on!" Emily pulls me to the door. "Time is money, honey!"

We run down the path toward Hunter, who's leaning against his car, the doors open and waiting for us. He kisses me on the cheek and tells me to get in.

"I promised your father I wouldn't drive over the

speed limit," he says. "But I didn't figure you'd spend so long inside gabbing."

"Sorry," I say breathlessly, climbing in. I look back up at the house and see Tom and Sonia crowding in the doorway with my parents, all of them waving good-bye like maniacs.

"Break an ankle!" Tom shouts as Hunter pulls away.

"I think he means me," says Hunter, giving a mock frown, and the three of us all start laughing. A few days ago, I thought I'd never be able to laugh like this again. Things haven't really changed—Miss Sara is still gone. But I'm so happy to have this chance to make her proud, just like my mother told me.

The train takes forever—some express service!—so Emily and I arrive at the Pavilion Theater just before two, both of us out of breath from running and from excitement. Far from being annoyed about changing our plans, Emily is really buzzed about being in the city today.

"I couldn't believe my parents agreed," she says as we wait for the light to change in Times Square. "Your mother just railroaded them. She told them she couldn't go with you herself, and I was the only person she could trust." Emily points up at the huge Broadway billboards. "Look, G—*The Lion King*! *Beauty and the Beast*! It's like we've been dropped in the center of the theater universe."

We'd spent most of the train ride chattering about what we'd do after the audition finished. This is going to be the best Diamond Day ever, that's certain. Rather than just watching *Breakfast at Tiffany's,* we're going to go to the *actual* Tiffany's and take pictures of each other outside. And speaking of photos, Emily even offered to take pictures of me so I can use them as head shots for future auditions.

"I'm getting pretty good, if I do say so myself," she said.

"I believe it," I told her, pleased that my auditioning for shows is something we can share, not something that has to jeopardize our friendship.

At least now I know where to find the stage door of the theater. A different guard is on duty today, and he checks my name off a list before admitting us. The grubby corridor seems almost familiar to me now, and I feel so much more confident clattering up the stairs, especially now that I'm not stuck in a line of hundreds of other girls. Emily and I follow his directions, and we end up not in a room like last time, but in the wings of the main stage.

"Oh my God," Emily whispers. We stand looking around at the towering backs of scenery, both open-mouthed. After the low-ceilinged corridor, it feels like we stepped into a cathedral. High above us, spotlights on tracks form a huge grid that extends across the stage. It's not totally dark back here—I guess at least some of the houselights are on—but it's so gloomy, especially with the black-painted floors, that suddenly I feel like it's evening rather than noon. I can only see slivers of the stage, but I can hear a girl singing on the other side of the scenery panels, with a piano plunking away in accompaniment. A number of people are milling about, and a woman wearing a headset bustles over to us.

"Grace Giovanni?" she asks, frowning at her list.

"Grace *di* Giovanni," I tell her, and the woman scribbles something onto the paper.

"They're running a little late," she says in a low voice. "There's still one girl before you. Got your music?"

I nod and grope for it in my bag, hoping I didn't drop it on the train. Thank goodness it's still there.

"Your friend will have to wait in the corridor," says the woman, not unkindly. "It's a rule—sorry. We have to keep the stage mothers at bay."

Emily and I give each other wistful looks, and she retreats through the door. I stand glued to the spot, trying to get my thoughts focused. For the first time, I notice the two girls auditioning before me, though I don't recognize either of them from the last time. I wish Chessy were here. I wouldn't even mind seeing that mean girl from my group. At least she would be a familiar face.

The other girl who's waiting glances at me and then looks away. She's wearing ballet practice gear, her dark hair pulled back into a severe bun, and I have a brief moment of panic, in case they're going to ask us to learn a dance routine on the spot. It's not that I don't like dancing—it's one of my favorite things, and the years of ballet training that my father is always complaining about because it cost him an arm and a leg mean I feel pretty confident about learning dance numbers. But I'm in such a fog right now, it's all I can do to focus on singing, let alone dancing up a storm as well.

The girl who was just onstage comes padding into the wings clutching her sheet music, heading straight for the door. Calm down, Grace, I tell myself. All they want us to do today is sing. And this time it won't be in a small, crowded room with bad acoustics and no accompaniment. I'll be standing on the stage—an actual Broadway stage!—with a pianist to keep me on track.

"Larissa Bean," calls a voice from the stage, and the ballet girl hurries out. My heart starts pounding, because this means I'm next. I earned this spot, I tell myself sternly. I came to the open audition, and then I got the callback. These big-time producers wouldn't have asked me here if they didn't think I had talent. But it's hard not to feel like an impostor standing here in the wings, with all these theater professionals hovering nearby. After all, I'm just a high school girl from Cumberland, Connecticut, with one lead role in a school production to my name. I bet ballet girl has performed on the stage thousands of times before.

She starts her song, a number I don't recognize. Her voice is clear and true, and she sounds like a professional. Really, I think I'm going to hyperventilate. What if my old stage fright returns? What if I get out onstage and just collapse in a heap? Sure, I was okay at school this year, but this is a much bigger deal. I close my eyes and hang my head, wishing I could sink through the floor.

And then I hear Miss Sara's voice telling me to pull myself together. *Miss-di-Gio-vanni*, she says, *this is your moment to shine. Do not be afraid of the brightness of your own star. Harness that power!*

I think about all the people who believe in me. My parents, who drove themselves crazy getting me back into this audition. My brother and sister, who were there to wave me off and wish me luck. Mrs. Lane, who wasted half her day yesterday, probably, making calls on my behalf. Nick Smart, who wanted me to audition for this show in the first place. Emily, my best friend, who's probably pacing in the corridor right now, willing me to do well. And Hunter, who understood at last what all this means to me and insisted on driving us to the station just to show his support. When he dropped us off, while Emily ran to get tickets, Hunter gathered me up in his arms.

"If I have to share you with your fans one day," he said, gazing into my eyes in a way that made me feel weak at the knees, "then I guess I'll have to learn how to deal with it."

The piano stops. Larissa has finished her song. Any second now she's going to walk offstage and then someone will call my name.

Stand up straight, Miss Sara would tell me. *Stride onto that stage with your head held high. Let them know they're looking at a star of the future.*

"Grace di Giovanni!"

I step forward.

"Hold on a second," the man who called my name tells me. We wait while Larissa walks toward us, looking very pale. She doesn't meet my eye as she passes. "Okay—hand your music to the pianist and then stand on the mark—see?"

I nod and take a deep breath. On the far side of the stage sits the rehearsal piano, and the redheaded man who's been playing is standing up, taking a long drink from a bottle of water. The mark is a black cross of tape in the middle of the stage, just a few feet from the edge. A spotlight is trained on it, forming a bright circle of light.

"You're on," says the man, gesturing toward the

piano, and I step out onto the stage, conscious of the boards creaking beneath my feet, of the huge expanse of empty theater to my right. I walk straight over to the pianist and hand him my music. He nods and shuffles it into position. Then, slowly, I walk to the black mark and stand looking out into the theater. A group of people are sitting way, way in the back, and with the light shining in my eyes, I can't even tell how many of them there are. All I can see is a blur of seats, elaborate racks of lights, the gilt decorations, and the red EXIT signs at the back of the theater. I've never sung on a stage as big as this, or in a theater this vast.

"Grace, right?" calls a man's voice from far away.

"Yes," I say, blinking, trying to steady my breathing.

"When you're ready," he says. I turn my head and nod to the pianist, and he plays the first bars. I stare out into the mostly empty rows, feeling the heat of the spotlight. I stand tall and hold my head high. This is it—my moment to shine—and I'm ready.